Trent's arms were around her, his lips descending, before she could guess his intention.

Fire flashed along her nerve endings at the first touch of his hot mouth against her skin. She gasped as his lips trailed down her throat. In the space of one heartbeat, she transitioned from wary to wonderful. His teeth grazed the sensitive joining of neck and shoulder and her toes curled. He knew her weaknesses. Every single one. Obviously he intended to capitalize on her bad judgment.

So what?

It had always been like this between them. Hot. Delicious. Inescapable. She groaned, surrendering to pleasure. Why not? They were both consenting adults. She was no longer married to his brother. She'd discovered the folly in trying to create a traditional family. Failing at that, what more did she have to lose by giving in to this rush of desire? And if she convinced Trent to help her in the process, what was the harm in that?

She wanted him, needed this. Why deny it? Later she could chastise herself for this rash act.

The Black She
Harlequin De
     Billic
Powerful
   their babies' little king

Dear Reader,

I'm delighted to be back in Las Vegas for *The Black Sheep's Secret Child*, and it was nice to revisit some characters from my original Las Vegas Nights series to see what they're up to. I'd like to thank my senior editor, Stacy Boyd, for suggesting a series set in the fascinating world of Vegas nightclubs. The first book in the Club T's Las Vegas Nights series, which is also a Billionaires and Babies novel, is both a reunion and a secret baby story. I hope you enjoy Savannah and Trent's second chance at love.

Happy reading,

Cat Schield

CAT SCHIELD

THE BLACK SHEEP'S SECRET CHILD

ISBN-13: 978-0-373-73487-0

The Black Sheep's Secret Child

Copyright © 2016 by Catherine Schield

This edition published by arrangement with Harlequin Books S.A.

For questions and comments about the quality of this book, please contact us at CustomerService@Harlequin.com.

Printed in U.S.A.

www.Harlequin.com

Cat Schield has been reading and writing romance since high school. Although she graduated from college with a BA in business, her idea of a perfect career was writing books for Harlequin. And now, after winning the Romance Writers of America 2010 Golden Heart® Award for Best Contemporary Series Romance, that dream has come true. Cat lives in Minnesota with her daughter, Emily, and their Burmese cat. When she's not writing sexy, romantic stories for Harlequin Desire, she can be found sailing with friends on the St. Croix River, or in more exotic locales, like the Caribbean and Europe. She loves to hear from readers. Find her at catschield.com. Follow her on Twitter, @catschield.

Books by Cat Schield

Harlequin Desire

The Black Sheep's Secret Child
Nanny Makes Three

The Sherdana Royals

Royal Heirs Required
A Royal Baby Surprise
Secret Child, Royal Scandal

Las Vegas Nights

At Odds with the Heiress
A Merger by Marriage
A Taste of Temptation

Visit her Author Profile page at Harlequin.com, or catschield.com, for more titles!

For my Desirable sisters, Jules, Sarah and Andrea.
You inspire me every day with your fabulousness.

One

Savannah Caldwell bypassed the line of partygoers held in a queue by velvet ropes and headed for the burly linebacker with the crooked nose guarding the nightclub's front entrance. Club T's was only open Friday through Monday. Without a table reservation, the average wait for general admission on a Monday night was one to three hours. Savannah had no intention of standing around that long to get in to see her brother-in-law.

A driving beat poured from the club's mirror-lined doorway. At one o'clock in the morning, Club T's was in full swing, and Savannah was actively second-guessing her impulse to hunt down Trent to discuss business at this unorthodox hour. But she'd been turned away from his office earlier when she'd tried to make an appointment with his assistant, and so coming here

seemed the only way she could get him to acknowledge her.

A wave of melancholy caught her off guard. She'd
been fixated on Trent since age eleven when she'd left
Tennessee and moved to LA to live with her aunt Stacy,
the Caldwell family's live-in housekeeper. At first Savannah had just wanted him to like her. As she entered high school, she'd developed a full-blown crush
on him. But it wasn't until she'd moved to New York
City at eighteen and began modeling that Trent finally
noticed her as a woman.

When she'd married Trent's brother, Rafe, sixteen
months ago, Trent had severed all contact with her.
The loss had been devastating. To cope she'd buried
her sadness. But suppressing her emotions had turned
her into a poorly crafted replica of who she used to
be. She spoke less. Dressed and acted like a matron
twice her age. She'd lost all touch with the optimistic
young woman who dreamed of a loving family, and a
husband who adored her.

Savannah stepped up to the blond bouncer with the
well-defined cheekbones. In four-inch heels, she stood
six feet tall, yet the top of her head came no higher than
the second button of his snug black polo with Club T's
logo. Where ten minutes ago she'd been truly determined, she was suddenly awash in hesitation. Even if
Savannah was comfortable with confrontation, she was
no match for this man. He was accustomed to subduing
intoxicated, belligerent troublemakers twice her size.

WWCD. What would Courtney do?

She drew in a breath to counteract her rising anxiety and ran through the centering exercises her acting coach had drilled into her. Playing the part of wealthy mean girl Courtney Day on a soap opera for three years had enabled Savannah to summon the demanding character at will, even two years after she'd stopped acting.

In the early days of working on the show, Savannah had struggled in a role as foreign to her as Courtney. While she'd certainly encountered enough rich, entitled and manipulative women during her years of living in the Caldwell household to draw from to create Courtney, Savannah hated the sort of conflict the socialite thrived on. Savannah would rather retreat than stick up for herself and had a hard time acting as if everyone should rush to do her bidding.

She'd landed the role because of how she'd looked in Courtney's designer clothes, with her hair and makeup done by professionals, not because she could act. Within the first two days, it was obvious she was going to be fired unless she learned to embrace Courtney's mean-girl persona. A fellow actor recommended her acting coach. Bert Shaw was tough and smart. He convinced her to live the persona 24/7 until she was more familiar with Courtney than Savannah. It had taken two weeks, but once she surrendered to Courtney's strengths, her flaws were easier to accept.

With a slow blink, Savannah wrapped herself in her alter ego once more. "I need to speak with Trent," she told the gatekeeper.

To her shock, the man nodded. The smile he gave her was surprisingly gentle for one of his imposing bulk. "Of course, Mrs. Caldwell. He said to let you right in."

Savannah wasn't sure whether to be delighted or worried that Trent had at long last made himself available after ignoring her phone calls for the last seven days. What sort of game was he playing? Knowing Trent the way she did, it could be any number of things.

"He'll be in the VIP section upstairs." The bouncer unhooked the rope from the stanchion and gestured her toward the entrance.

Courtney treated most people as if they existed only to serve her. Savannah should have sailed through without giving the bouncer another glance, but she sent him a grateful smile as she went by.

Once upon a time she might have enjoyed being here, but not tonight. Club T's catered to twentysomethings who favored short dresses that bared long tanned legs and impressive amounts of cleavage. As she eased through the press of bodies, she was feeing positively archaic.

She'd had fun taking in the LA and New York City nightlife at Trent's side. But that was before she'd entered a loveless marriage, given birth to her son and become a widow all in the space of a year and a half. Not what she'd hoped for herself.

When she thought about the girl who'd dreamed of living happily ever after, she missed her a lot. Naive and very foolish she might have been, but she'd also been brimming with optimism. Undaunted by a lonely childhood where she'd been more burden than someone's pride and joy, she'd craved a traditional family lifestyle, with a husband and children, a cozy house with a dog, and a white picket fence. Instead, she'd fallen for Trent Caldwell and picked the one man who would never make her dreams come true…

Handsome and confident, with an irresistible charm, Trent could also be difficult and moody when things didn't go his way. His family brought out the worst in him, something Savannah had often witnessed during the years she'd lived with them.

When Trent's father, Siggy, went after his younger son for his wild nature and reckless behavior, the whole house had resonated with his denigrating monologues. Siggy saw himself as the head of a dynasty and viewed Trent as the bad seed. During the seven years Savannah had lived with her aunt, it became clear that while eldest son, Rafe, could do no wrong, younger son, Trent, did nothing right.

In the aftermath of those arguments, Savannah had always gone to Trent. In him she saw reflected the loneliness and isolation that defined her situation. Believing they were kindred spirits fanned her girlish crush on him. She supposed that Trent acted the way he did because it was expected of him rather than because it was his nature. Just as she was confident that if he'd been raised by a father who'd been supportive and kind, rather than a tyrant, he would have ended up totally different.

She paused at the edge of the dance floor and searched for the stairs that would take her into the VIP section. Since Savannah had never visited Las Vegas before, she had no idea where she was going. The photographs she'd seen of Club T's didn't do the enormity of the place justice. The club occupied forty thousand square feet in Cobalt, one of the premier hotels on the Strip. In addition to the enormous dance floor inside, the club boasted a sprawling outdoor patio and pool area.

The club was owned by three men—the T's that made up the club's name. Trent Caldwell, Savannah's brother-in-law, who managed the day-to-day business, had a 50 percent stake. The other half was split between Kyle Tailor, former Cubs pitcher and part owner of the LA Dodgers as well as the boyfriend of Trent's sister, Melody, and Nate Tucker, Grammy-winning singer/songwriter, Free Fall's lead singer, producer and owner of Ugly Trout Records.

Before Savannah could start moving again, a medium-size man with brown hair snagged her arm. "Hey, there, beautiful. If you're looking for someone, here I am. Let me buy you a drink."

"No, thank you."

"Come on. One drink."

"I'm meeting someone."

"I'm sure he won't mind."

She'd had too many encounters with men like this. She didn't need a basket filled with cookies or a red cape to attract the wolves. Something beyond being blonde and pretty made her prey. And all too often she had a tendency to trust when she should question instead.

"I mind."

The bodies around them shifted, allowing Savannah to slip away without further confrontation. She angled away from the bar and the dance floor. Sheer luck allowed her to blunder in the right direction. Another mammoth guarded the VIP entrance, but he let her in without challenge. Noting the earpiece he wore, Savannah assumed he'd been warned to expect her.

She wound her way past plush, curved couches loaded with celebrities from the music industry and Hollywood. Her brother-in-law was easy to locate. She just needed to look for the most beautiful women.

Trent was completely in his element. Like an emperor accustomed to being adored, he sat on a curved couch, arms spread wide to allow the brunettes flanking him to snuggle close. Each girl had a drink in one hand and rested the other hand possessively on Trent. If they hoped to pin down this elusive bachelor, Savannah wished them luck. From the look on his face, he wasn't into either of them. Not that that would stop him from showing them a good time. And from their blatant pawing, it appeared that's what they were looking for.

Savannah stepped up to Trent's table and spoke his name. The DJ picked that second to talk over the loud music and drowned out her voice. Nevertheless, whether he heard his name or just noticed her awkwardly standing there, Trent turned his attention to her.

As his eyes met hers, longing slammed into her, as inescapable as it was four years ago when he'd kissed her for the first time. Strong emotions bumped up her heart rate and released butterflies in her stomach. Squaring her shoulders, she ignored her body's disloyalty. She couldn't let Trent get to her. She'd come to Las Vegas with a business proposition and that's what she needed to focus on.

"Savannah, what a surprise." A welcoming smile curved his lips, but to someone who'd seen Trent unguarded and truly happy, it looked fake. "Come join us."

She shook her head. "I'm not here to party."

He mimed that he couldn't hear her and waved her closer. Savannah held her ground, not relishing the idea of becoming one of his groupies. If she'd felt out of place downstairs, that was nothing compared to the humiliation of standing on display for Trent's fashion-forward friends. Pity, boredom and mockery made up their expressions as they judged her.

In the year and a half since she and Rafe had become a couple, she'd adapted to his preferred style. Her husband had dictated that she wear her hair sleek and fill her closet with elegant clothes worthy of a CEO's wife. Tonight, she'd been thinking along the lines of business rather than clubbing when she'd left the suite wearing a sheath of red satin and sheer checkerboard squares over a nude lining. It covered her from collarbone to knee and made her stand out from the crowd in the worst way possible.

"I need to speak to you." As much as she hated raising her voice, the loud dance music required her to shout to be heard.

"Just one drink." He signaled the waitress. "One drink and we can talk right here."

She was not going to go sit beside Trent and pretend that the way he'd treated her this last year and a half hadn't bothered her. Because it had. She'd been angry with Trent for refusing to even consider making a commitment to her and tormented by guilt for marrying his brother for all the wrong reasons.

Savannah crossed her arms over her chest. She might have to beg for Trent's help, but she wouldn't let him see her humiliation at needing to do so.

"I'd prefer our conversation to be a private one."

She'd never negotiated with Trent and won. The man never seemed to care whether or not he got what he wanted. He was always ready to walk away from the bargaining table, which gave him an advantage.

They stared at each other—each determined to have their way—until the music and the lights faded to insignificance in the background. Trent's gaze toured her body with lazy intensity as he waited for her to surrender to his will. It bothered Savannah how much she wanted to give in to him.

His power over her hadn't faded one bit. Her thoughts were jumbled as she was overwhelmed by the urge to taste his sexy mouth and feel his hands roaming all over her. Their lovemaking had always been hot and satisfying. He'd spent an exceptional amount of time getting to know her body's every sensitive spot. An ache blossomed inside her. It had been nineteen long months since she'd last been with him, and her every nerve was on fire with anticipation.

Coming here tonight had been a bad idea. She should have held out for a civilized meeting in his office. Instead, she was filled with a recklessness inspired by the dance music's heavy beat and her own dangerous desire.

She had to go.

As a child Savannah had coped with her father's temper and her grandmother's frequent illnesses by hiding somewhere she felt safe. By the time she'd become a teenager, the habit of fleeing difficult situations was fully ingrained in her psyche. Retreat and regroup. Now that she was a mother, she'd grown better at standing her ground, but when overly stressed she fell back on what was familiar. Which explained why she turned away from Trent and headed for the exit.

The club seemed busier than it had five minutes earlier. Savannah wormed through the press of undulating bodies, familiar tightness building in her chest. The ever-changing lights and the hammering beat of the music combined to batter her senses. Her legs shook as she wound her way past the dance floor, and she wrenched her ankle during an awkward sidestep. Her head began to spin. Pressure built until she wanted to scream. She had to get out of the club. But which direction was the exit?

"There you are." The man she'd escaped earlier sneaked his arm around her waist and breathed alcohol at her. Her brief encounter with Trent had stripped away her Courtney armor. Locked in her panic attack, she was vulnerable to the man's boldness. "Thought you could get away from me, didn't you?" His lips met her cheek in an untidy kiss.

"Let me go," she said, but her voice lacked energy and the man was too drunk to hear her even if she'd shouted.

"Let's dance."

"No." She tried to squirm away but found nowhere to escape as the crowd pressed in on them.

All at once a large hand landed on the man's shoulder and tightened. With a yelp, the guy set her free.

"Hey, man. What are you doing?"

The drunk might have been a wolf, but Trent was a ferocious lion. "Leave this club before I have you thrown out."

If she hadn't been so rattled, Savannah might have enjoyed the way her assailant scrambled away from Trent.

Despite the heat being generated by a thousand dancers, Savannah's skin prickled with goose bumps. The urge to turn tail and run seized her, but before the impulse worked its way into her muscles, Trent slipped his arm around her waist.

Through modeling Savannah had gained an understanding of her physical appeal. Training to become Courtney Day had shown her how to act more confident. By the time Trent had come to New York to visit his sister, Melody, at Juilliard, Savannah was no longer an insecure girl, but a confident, sensual woman he desired. And more importantly, one he could have.

Falling back into old patterns with Trent was easy and comfortable, and she didn't resist as he drew her away from the crowd. He led her to a nondescript door, used a key card to activate the electronic lock and maneuver her through.

As the door clicked shut behind them, leaving them alone in a brightly lit hallway, Trent brushed her ear with his lips. "I see you still need someone to watch over you."

Being in his debt before she'd asked for his help

wasn't a successful approach. "You didn't give me the chance to handle him."

"Would you like me to fetch him back?"

Savannah fought to control a shiver, knowing that to give in was to let him know how much she appreciated being rescued. "No."

Trent smirked at her. "You said you wanted a private conversation. How private do you need it to be?"

"Somewhere we can talk uninterrupted." She glanced up and down the twenty-foot hallway, seeing no one but hearing voices and laughter from around a corner.

"My office is quiet," he said, fingers sliding along her spine in a tantalizing caress. "Unless you're afraid to be alone with me?"

She twitched as his touch sent a lance of pleasure through her. "Why would I be?"

"You're quivering." He nuzzled her hair, voice deep and intimate. "Makes me think of the last time we were alone together."

"That was almost two years ago." But already the increased agitation in her hormones signaled that the chemistry between them remained as combustible as ever. *Damn.* She hadn't counted on lust being a factor in her negotiations with Trent.

"In the past, we've had a hard time keeping our hands off each other."

"That explains why you stayed away from me. Why did you stop taking Rafe's phone calls? It really hurt him."

His blue eyes narrowed. "Ask me if I'm worried how Rafe felt. He was my older brother, yet he never once stood up for me against Siggy. Not when we were kids or when Siggy refused to bring me into the family business. Rafe was the golden child and he liked it that way. So, what? I'm supposed to forgive and forget because he has a change of heart on his deathbed?"

There it was. That chip on his shoulder. The one he'd developed in response to every slight his father had delivered. Trent had been the second son. The spare heir. The boy with eclectic musical interests and strong opinions.

She couldn't disagree with his perception of his relationship with his brother and father. She'd heard the arguments. They didn't appreciate just how brilliant he was. The only opinions Siggy Caldwell entertained were his own. Rafe had learned about the business at his father's knee, never challenging Siggy's decisions.

"Still want to talk?" Trent asked. Had he noticed something in her manner that led him to believe she regretted coming here tonight?

"Yes."

"Good. I'm dying to hear what brought you to Las Vegas."

"I need your help."

"You must be pretty desperate if you came to me." Trent scrutinized her expression for a beat before taking her by the arm and leading her down the hall. "Let's go to my office. You can tell me all about it."

As soon as Trent escorted Savannah into his office and closed the door behind them, he knew this was a bad idea. He blamed curiosity. She'd been trying to get a hold of him for a week.

Yet, he could've picked up the phone at any time and

discovered what was on her mind. But he'd resisted. What had changed?

Long-buried emotions, aroused by the familiar scent of her perfume, provided the answer. His fingers itched to slide over her smooth skin. From his first sight of her in the club tonight, he'd been fighting the longing to back her against a wall and ease his mouth over her quaking body.

He released her arm and turned his back to her. Picturing her naked and moaning his brother's name reminded him why he'd been keeping his distance.

He slipped behind a wet bar that ran perpendicular to the wall of floor-to-ceiling monitors tuned to various key areas in the club. Fixing her a drink gave him something useful to do until the urge to crush her mouth beneath his abated. Trent gave himself a hard mental shake. Obviously he hadn't thought through this scenario when he'd suggested they use his office for their private conversation. Being alone with Savannah shouldn't trigger his libido. He thought he'd gotten over her the instant she'd said "I do" to his brother. Damn if he'd been wrong.

Disgusted, Trent pulled a bottle from the fridge and surveyed the label. "Champagne?" When she shook her head, he arched an eyebrow. "Aren't we celebrating?"

Her frown asked, *Celebrating what?* "You know I don't drink."

"Oh," he drawled. "I thought perhaps after being married to my brother, you might have started."

Savannah made a face at him but didn't rise to the bait. "I'll take some sparkling water if you have it."

Amused, Trent dropped ice into a glass and poured her a drink. Fixing a lime to the rim, he pushed the glass across the bar toward her. As much as he could use a scotch to settle his nerves, he refrained. Dealing with Savannah was complicated enough without a fuzzy head.

A familiar mixture of fondness and rage filled him as he watched her sip the drink.

From the moment the naive eleven-year-old with the big blue eyes had moved into the servants' quarters of his family's Beverly Hills home, he'd been drawn to her. Unlike his twelve-year-old sister, she'd exhibited none of the gawkiness of preteen girls. And her lack of street smarts had driven Trent crazy.

As a kid he'd slipped into rebellious and resentful mode pretty early. Being a troublemaker came easy. He wasn't anyone's hero. But he'd come to Savannah's rescue more times than he could count. She'd been a magnet for anyone eager to take advantage of a young girl from some backwoods town in Tennessee. To look at her you'd think she would turn to smoke if you touched her, but in fact there was supple muscle beneath her soft skin, something he'd discovered firsthand when he'd taught her a couple self-defense moves.

In some ways, she was still the same ragamuffin who'd needed protection from the mean girls in school and the boys who thought to take advantage of her naïveté. But being on her own in New York had given her a new set of skills. For one, she'd learned how to go after something she wanted. And for a while it was pretty apparent that what she'd wanted was him.

Which was why it had come as such a surprise that she'd chosen to marry his brother. Despite the years she'd spent in LA and New York, she remained a small-town girl at heart. She had no lofty dreams of fame and fortune. She'd never known stability growing up, so as an adult, Savannah craved marriage and children, a secure, safe life.

Her vision of a traditional family situation was completely foreign to Trent. His father was an ambitious tyrant who'd married late. His misogynistic behavior had driven his wife away not long after Melody was born. The prenup their mother had signed granted her nothing if she fought for custody of her children. Trent had never been surprised that she'd chosen the money.

Was it any wonder he had so little interest in marriage and family? But knowing how important it was to Savannah should've warned him to keep his distance. He might have, but she was irresistible to him.

No matter how many times he'd cautioned himself to stay away, he couldn't stop coming to her rescue. Only once had he abandoned her to trouble—the day she'd declared her intention to marry Rafe.

"Widowhood becomes you," he said. If he'd hoped to shock her, he failed.

Reproachful blue eyes fixed on him. "That's a terrible thing to say."

"Perhaps, but it doesn't stop it from being true."

Young Savannah had possessed a guilelessness that left her open for the world to read. And take advantage of. He'd expected her to be eaten alive in the cutthroat world of modeling and acting in New York City, but she'd figured out a way to survive. When he'd visited Melody during her junior year at Juilliard, he'd been checking in on Savannah, as well. At first he'd been surprised. The naive girl wasn't gone, but she'd become a little wiser. She'd also gained an air of mystery. He'd been intrigued.

He still was.

"Perhaps you should tell me why you're here, dear sister-in-law."

Her lips formed a moue of distaste at the specific emphasis he put on the last three words. Trent took no pleasure in highlighting the chasm between them, but it needed to be done.

"I have a proposition for you."

Trent had been dodging her for a week, assuming something of this sort. For sixteen months he'd been waiting for her to admit that marrying his brother had been a mistake. It irritated him that she hadn't. And now she wanted something from him.

"I'm not interested."

"You haven't even heard me out."

"We have nothing to talk about."

Her facial muscles tightened, lending her expression a determined look he'd never seen before. She'd always seemed untouched by demons that drove most people, unfazed by success or obstacles. What had changed? Marriage to his brother? Motherhood?

These were questions best left alone. Trent didn't need to venture down the rabbit hole of turbulent emotions conjured whenever he spent time with Savannah. Better to speed her on her way back to LA and be done with temptation.

"Maybe we don't have anything to talk about, but *I* have a great deal to say."

"Why don't you make an appointment with my office for some time next week." He knew he was taunting her but couldn't help himself. She'd become another in a long list of people who brought out his bad side.

"I've already been here five days and you've been avoiding me. I'm closing on the sale of my house tomorrow afternoon, so Dylan and I are leaving in the morning. I had hoped to have everything settled before we returned to LA."

Against his better judgment—because he was playing directly into her hands—Trent asked, "What exactly did you intend to have settled?"

"When Rafe died, he left his shares of West Coast Records to Dylan. That means until Dylan's eighteenth birthday, I'm in charge of the business." She shook her head. "I need help."

Now Trent was starting to see where she was going. "You've got Gerry." Gerry Brueger had been Siggy's second in command for twenty years. Passed over for president when Siggy stepped down and installed Rafe as the head of the company, Gerry would jump at the chance to take over.

"It's not that simple. I need a CEO I can trust. Someone who gets the business and can turn things around."

"So hire someone."

"That's what I'm trying to do." She cocked her head and scowled at him.

"Me?" This was not at all what he'd expected. Trent shook his head. "Not interested."

"It's your family's company."

"It's my *father's* company." And his brother's. They'd never wanted him to be a part of it. "Besides, my father isn't going to welcome my interference." He noticed that her gaze shifted away. "Have you talked to Siggy about this?"

"It's my decision." But she sounded less confident than she'd been moments earlier.

"So you haven't mentioned any of this to Siggy?"

"He sold a majority of his shares in the business to Rafe. Dylan inherited them. Siggy isn't in control of the company anymore."

Her naïveté was showing. She might think she was in charge, but she was in for a huge battle if she thought she could bring Trent into the record company. He almost felt sorry for her.

"Sell the company back to Siggy and wash your hands of it."

"It's not that cut-and-dried." She set her untouched glass of water on a nearby table and squared her shoulders. "He won't buy back Rafe's shares, but I know he's planning to control things behind the scenes. Siggy intends for Dylan to run the company someday." Savannah paused and compressed her lips into a thin line. With a sigh, she continued, "In the meantime, I can't run it and I don't trust your father to be able to turn things around."

"Turn things around?" Trent had heard rumblings that West Coast Records was having financial problems. No surprise there—Siggy Caldwell's approach to the music industry was uninspired and his eldest son had been a chip off the old block. "What's going on?"

"I'm not exactly sure, because I've been getting the runaround from Gerry, but I think they're behind on paying royalties to their artists."

"When did this start?"

"I don't know. Shortly after we were married, Rafe confided to me that the company was struggling financially before your father retired." That had occurred three years earlier. "And after the cancer started eating away at Rafe, he wasn't making the best decisions. I'm sure things got much worse then."

Trent ignored the compulsion that demanded he step in and fix everything. "While this is all fascinating, what does any of it have to do with me?"

"The company needs you." Her big blue eyes went soft and concerned in the way that always kicked him hard in the solar plexus.

Trent's first impulse was to laugh. He never got the chance. Questions crowded in. He didn't give a damn about the company. But did *she* need him? Trent crossed his arms over his chest and regarded her through half-closed eyes. She was beautiful. Poised. But not happy. He should've felt triumphant. Instead there was a dull ache in his gut.

"You know, better than most, that isn't going to sway me. Try again."

She gazed at the blank walls that made up his office. If she was looking for some clue about how to appeal to him, she wouldn't find it there. He was a man who didn't give a damn about anything. Or that's the face he showed the world. It made it much harder for someone to hurt him if he showed no vulnerability.

"Prove to your father you're a better businessman than he is."

He should be gloating. Trent—not his father or brother—would be the one to save the struggling West Coast Records, but his only emotion was bitterness.

"He would never believe that." The great Siggy Caldwell never owned up to his mistakes. He sure as hell wouldn't admit that his pitiful excuse for a second son was a better anything. "If that's the best you have, I'm afraid I'm going to have to disappoint you."

She let the silence fill the space between them for a beat before speaking. "I need your help."

He resisted the urge to sweep her into his arms and pledge his support. She was staring at him in desperate hope, as if he was her knight in shining armor. That was the farthest thing from reality. Sure, maybe he'd helped her out a time or two in the past, but she wasn't his responsibility anymore. The time for rescuing her had ended sixteen months earlier when she'd promised to love, honor and cherish his brother.

"And just like that, you expect me to drop everything and rush to your aid?" It cost him, but he gave his words a sardonic twist and hardened his heart. "It's not going to happen."

Two

Despite all the times he'd rescued her in the past, Savannah knew she shouldn't have counted on Trent helping her. She'd committed the ultimate sin. She'd married his brother.

And now she was stuck in an untenable position. Her one-year-old son had inherited stock she couldn't sell to a third party without her father-in-law's permission. This meant as an asset it held no value for her. And because of the way the record label was hemorrhaging money, the stock would be worthless in no time.

Begging to be rescued was too humiliating and probably wouldn't work anyway. Negotiating was a much more palatable option. Once again, she channeled Courtney Day. Relaxing her shoulders, she spoke in her alter ego's confident tone.

"What can I say or do to change your mind?"

"I don't know." Something flickered in Trent's eyes. "What are you offering?"

"I have nothing to bargain with."

Cards on the table, she maintained her poker face while his gaze raked over her. Heat rose to her skin. It wasn't humiliation she felt, but desire. If confronted, he would deny that he wanted her, but the flare of his nostrils and the way his pupils dilated hinted that the chemistry between them hadn't faded.

"You have something."

Savannah shook her head, unsure if what she was picking up off him was real or wishful thinking. "Rafe burned through all our cash chasing alternative medical treatments that didn't work," she said. "After he died, I had to sell the house to pay off his debts."

And she'd come up short by a million. She'd counted on selling Rafe's shares back to Siggy for enough money to clear the debt and maybe have a little bit to start over somewhere new.

But Siggy didn't want his shares back. He wanted Rafe's son.

"The only thing of value left is Dylan's shares in the company," she continued. "But I can't touch that."

"I don't want money," Trent said.

No, of course not. He could buy West Coast Records three times over. "What do you want?"

That she was putting herself in his hands occurred to her the instant the words were past her lips. But what else could she do? Siggy was willing to clear her debt but insisted she and Dylan move in with him. Her father-in-law's opinion of her was low. He hadn't approved of his son marrying her and he'd let her know that on several occasions. The thought of living in that toxic environment made her panic.

"Why did you marry my brother?"

The question came out of nowhere, and for several seconds Savannah didn't know what to say. Discussing her marriage with Trent was fraught with too many complications. Trent would never understand or approve of what she'd done, because he couldn't understand how her circumstances had left her feeling vulnerable and alone.

"You knew what I wanted. What was the most important thing to me."

Something Trent was never going to give her—a family. They stared at each other while her unspoken answer hung between them. Speaking of her longing would open up old wounds and she couldn't bear that.

I can't give you what you want.

Her heart had shattered when he'd uttered those words two years earlier.

At last she sighed. "I wanted to be married. To have children."

"I don't understand why you chose Rafe. Was it because you were pregnant?"

Savannah noticed he didn't ask her if she'd loved his brother. Why bother when the math was obvious? Dylan had been born six months after Savannah and Rafe had promised to love, honor and cherish each other until death.

"That played into it." She'd been devastated that the

man she loved couldn't give her what she wanted and terrified of raising a child on her own.

Why had she chosen Rafe? Because he'd wanted her.

"Rafe was excited about being a father. Family was important to him."

More important than she'd initially understood. And he'd been very persuasive. At the time she'd believed she could trust him. She wouldn't have married him if he'd been like Trent. But he'd never once made her doubt his desire to be a father, and he'd been over-the-moon excited that she was carrying a boy.

"Rafe and Siggy were exactly alike," Trent scoffed. "People mean no more to them than as a means to an end."

It was humiliating to know just how right Trent was about that. She'd thought Rafe was her friend. Growing up he'd been the nice one, always upbeat and well mannered. He'd never hurt Savannah's feelings when she'd tried to cheer him out of a bad mood. He'd been the one to lift her spirits.

From when they were kids, he'd known how she felt about his brother. A couple times he'd come upon her crying in the midst of teenage angst over Trent. And he'd made her feel less unwanted.

Rafe had been the one who'd encouraged her to take the modeling job in New York. And after she quit the soap opera and returned to LA, he'd been the one who'd helped her find a rental.

She'd never questioned why Rafe was so accepting about the circumstances surrounding her pregnancy. Nor had her suspicions been aroused by the fact that he'd been the one who'd handed her a box of condoms and sent her to Las Vegas to visit Trent and get him out of her system once and for all.

It wasn't until after Dylan was born, when Rafe collapsed and she discovered the illness he'd been hiding, that she'd learned how he'd tricked her. That he'd sabotaged the box of condoms. Gambled that she would get pregnant.

He'd bought into his father's notions of a dynasty. Wanted a son, but his cancer treatments had left him impotent and sterile. So he'd taken a chance and tricked her into getting pregnant by his brother.

At first she'd been shocked and appalled at being manipulated by someone she trusted. But in the end she couldn't hate a man who'd made such poor decisions with a death sentence hanging over his head.

"That last time we were together," Trent began, his voice pitched low. "Were you and Rafe already involved?"

Savannah came out of her musing to find Trent standing within arm's reach. Closer than she'd expected. He stood with his head cocked, his manner watchful, as if waiting for a sign from her. Suddenly she was having trouble catching her breath.

He hadn't touched her. He showed no inclination that he wanted to. So why was she suddenly craving his kiss?

"Does it matter?" She should back away. Put the width of the room between them. A table. A chair. Better yet, a door. Several corridors. A couple dozen floors.

"Not to me." His tone was light but his gaze was intense. "But my brother might have appreciated knowing you were cheating on him with me."

"I wasn't cheating on him. With you or anyone else."

In her rush to vindicate herself in his eyes, she neglected to remember that little matter of math. Would Trent realize that nine months after they had been together in Las Vegas, she'd given birth to Dylan? The thought terrified her. What if he wouldn't help her after discovering she'd kept the truth about his son from him? It was a practical concern, but not her bigger fear.

It hadn't taken a lot for Rafe to convince her that once Trent learned the truth that he would still reject her and his son.

Which is why she hadn't told him about Dylan when she'd discovered she was pregnant. Was it cowardly of her to hide the truth because she was assuming the worst outcome? Of course, but nothing Trent had ever said to her gave her reason to hope that he'd miraculously alter his way of thinking because he was going to be a father.

"I don't want to talk about my marriage."

"Then we've run out of things to say to each other." Trent gestured toward his office door.

"That isn't necessarily true," she countered, snatching at something to keep the conversation rolling. If she kept him talking, he wouldn't be able to throw her out of his office and maybe she could get the topic back around to the record label.

"What else did you have in mind?"

"You could ask me about Murphy."

He'd gotten her the French bulldog as a Christmas present three years ago. At the time she'd thought he'd bought the cream-colored snore monster because he was starting to get ideas of taking their relationship to the next level. She'd been in heaven.

Having Trent all to herself for those two weeks had been magical. They'd snuggled on the couch and opened presents at midnight on Christmas Eve. The week leading up to New Year's, they'd walked the puppy, browsed through Chinatown and the East Village, taken in a couple Broadway shows. They'd rung in the New Year with a bottle of champagne and the most perfect lovemaking of Savannah's life.

Then, six weeks later, he'd canceled on her last minute, and she'd spent Valentine's Day crying into Murphy's soft puppy coat. She'd realized that the long-distance thing wasn't working for her and she'd decided to quit the soap opera and move back to LA.

"How is he?"

"Wonderful. He's devoted to Dylan. Follows him everywhere. Curls up with him at nap time."

"How did Rafe enjoy sharing his bed with the dog?"

Questions like these were a minefield. How did she answer? She couldn't reveal that she'd entered into a loveless marriage and had never shared a bed with her husband.

"He didn't." Which was at least true.

"I'm not surprised. Rafe was never an animal person."

Unlike Trent, who'd fostered several rescues over the years. He liked helping out—something he'd deny—but the temporary nature of providing a home for dogs who after a couple months moved on to permanent situations demonstrated his unwillingness to commit and his distaste for being tied down.

She'd been so hurt by his refusal to move their relationship forward, even though she'd known that's how he was when she'd gotten involved with him. She kept hoping that he'd change. That she'd be the one he'd fall in love with and would be unable to live without.

Instead, in her sorrow and loss, she'd let his brother manipulate her. In her heart she'd known Trent was a better man than his brother, and a small part of her had expected him to save her one more time.

Only he hadn't. And she couldn't blame him for leaving her to rot.

"I'm sorry," she murmured.

"For what?"

"It was wrong of me to get involved with Rafe."

"I've been waiting a year and a half for you to admit that."

Trent's arms were around her, his lips descending, before she could guess his intention. Fire flashed along her nerve endings at the first touch of his hot mouth against her skin. She gasped as his lips trailed down her throat. In the space of one heartbeat, she transitioned from wary to wondrous. His teeth grazed the sensitive joining of neck and shoulder and her toes curled. He knew her weaknesses. Every single one. Obviously he intended to capitalize on her bad judgment.

So what?

It had always been like this between them. Hot. Delicious. Inescapable. She groaned, surrendering to pleasure. Why not? They were both consenting adults. She was no longer married to his brother. This had nowhere to go. She'd discovered the folly in trying to create a traditional family. Failing at that, what more did she have to lose by giving in to this rush of desire? And if she convinced Trent to help her in the process, what was the harm in that?

All these thoughts flashed through her head in the instant before Trent's hand slid over her butt and pulled her pelvis into snug contact with his arousal. She fisted her hands in his hair and tugged to bring his mouth to hers. She wanted him, needed this—why deny it? Later she could chastise herself for this rash act.

Trent captured her mouth in a hot, sizzling kiss. The ache between her thighs pulsed with more urgency as his tongue plunged past her teeth. She met the thrust with ardent fervor. A growl vibrated in her throat. That they could be discovered at any second should have bothered her. On the other hand, maybe Trent had entertained enough women in here to make his staff wary of interrupting their boss.

That thought too should have disturbed her. But Savannah was beyond logic and reason.

She drew him toward the couch and pushed him onto it. He bounced a little as the cushions gave beneath him. With a sassy grin, she hiked up her skirt and climbed onto his lap. Settling her hot center against his erection caused them both to shudder. She wasn't sure when the Courtney Day persona had fallen away. What she was doing now was pure Savannah.

Breath ragged, palms gliding up her thigh, he regarded her. His guards were up. He'd tightened his lips into an unyielding line and a sharp line appeared between his strong, dark brows. Questions gathered in his eyes. Savannah rocked her hips in a sultry move that caused him to exhale sharply in a low curse.

He started to speak. She shushed him and captured his face between her hands to keep him still while she flicked her tongue against his lower lip and then pulled it between her teeth and sucked gently. Strong fingers dug into her thighs hard enough to leave bruises. She smiled as she kept up the tantalizing seduction of his mouth.

Earlier when he'd pulled her against him, she'd felt the familiar square of tin that held breath mints and a little something extra in his suit coat pocket. Now she reached for the box and slipped it free. Trent heard the familiar rattle and leaned away from her kiss.

Savannah sat up straight and held the tin between them. "I see you haven't changed your habits."

"I like being prepared."

She popped the lid and slipped a mint into her mouth. Sharp and cool, the peppermint flavor exploded on her tongue, making it tingle. "Want one?"

Eyes locked on hers, he opened his mouth and let her feed him one. While the mint dissolved, they regarded each other in silence. His gaze held challenge, but curiosity, as well. He wanted to know if she intended to get to what else the tin held. Savannah savored his anticipation. He liked being in charge. It's why he hadn't stuck around to be a part of his family's business, but had struck out on his own.

No one was going to boss around Trent Caldwell.

But Savannah had found him to be a wonderful partner in bed. For as often as he'd swept her into his passion and demanded her surrender, there had always been opportunities when he let her take the lead. Because of this, her confidence had flourished, not only with regard to her sexuality, but also in her worth as an individual.

The heavy pulse of desire between her thighs hadn't diminished one bit during this exchange. In fact, as she grew more committed to this next step, her hunger for him had only increased.

Savannah plucked out the square foil package and held it up. "Only one? You used to carry at least two." She might have sounded confident, but she wasn't. Courtney Day might not have thought twice about a quickie with her sexy ex, but Savannah was rapidly losing her nerve.

"What makes you think I haven't used one already today?"

Trent had a healthy sexual appetite, and she wouldn't be surprised if he'd already had sex with three other women. She shouldn't care. But it hurt all the same. Several deep breaths later she'd pushed down panic and dismay. This couldn't become about what she'd had and lost. She needed a brief interlude to escape her troubles and there was no better man to rock her world than Trent.

But why was he baiting her? She could see from his flat stare that he expected her to back off.

"For a second I forgot who I was dealing with." She closed the tin with a metallic snap and tossed it aside.

Aware that he was scrutinizing her every move, she placed the wrapped condom between her teeth and set her hands to loosening his belt. Up until now she'd been doing a good job of appearing confident. But beneath Trent's unreadable gaze, she felt a tiny fizz of nervous energy dance along her spine, making her fingers clumsy. Trent made no attempt to help her. In fact he didn't move at all, except for the unsteady rise and fall of his chest.

At long last Savannah slid down his zipper and freed him. His erection sprang into her hands, eager for her attention. Overwhelmed by joy at what they were about to do, she paused for a moment, fingers coasting along his hot silken length. With a half smile she tore open the wrapper and unrolled the condom, sheathing him. His head had fallen back against the couch while his breath hissed out between clenched teeth. He squeezed his eyes shut and held perfectly still, every muscle in his body tense beneath her.

In her stylish but conservatively cut dress, Savannah might not have appeared as if she'd planned for a hot night at the club, but she'd chosen a red lace bra and thong set to wear underneath. Had she thought in her wildest dreams she would be in this position? Perhaps her subconscious had wanted this all along.

Before she could change her mind about what she was about to do, Savannah cupped Trent's erection in her palm, slid aside her thong and brought his tip into contact with her wet heat.

For the first time in several seconds Trent shifted. He cupped her butt in both hands and moved her forward and down until he was sheathed inside her. They groaned simultaneously as she came to rest, fully seated on his lap once again. Savannah put her hands on his shoulders, needing him for balance as her head began to spin.

This wasn't just sex. It had never been just sex between them. But there were no words of love or affectionate looks exchanged. This was a crazy, impulsive interlude that she desperately needed. Her goal was oblivion, and being with Trent always enabled her to forget her problems. Even when what was troubling her was Trent himself.

They rocked together in a familiar rhythm, maintaining a steady, relaxed pace.

"Take your hair down," Trent demanded, his voice an unsteady rasp.

Happy to oblige, she reached up and pulled out half a dozen pins and demolished the smooth, controlled hairstyle with a languid shake of her head. Long blond waves tumbled around her shoulders and tickled her cheeks. Trent had always loved her hair. He sank his fingers into the thick silky mass and brought her lips back to his.

Trent wasn't sure how he'd come to be on his couch buried deep inside Savannah, her tongue dancing with his in a passionate kiss, her manner every bit as wild as he remembered. Another woman might have pleaded with him for help or screamed abuse when he refused to fall in with her plans. He'd had only the briefest suspicion that Savannah intended to seduce him into helping her before he rejected the idea. Her hunger for him was as all-consuming as his for her.

That didn't make this a reunion between lovers. Not in the traditional sense. Sixteen months of bitter silence lay between them. Part of him didn't want to open the door to her. The part of him that did was in charge at the moment. Maybe what they were doing was saying goodbye. But as her teeth nipped at his lower lip, driving him closer to orgasm, he knew this brief taste of her had only revived his unquenchable desire.

Trent fought to make the moment last. But he was only able to hold on until he could determine that she hovered on the brink of a climax.

Her soft keening and the accelerated rhythm of her hips pushed him over the edge and they came together. Heart thundering, Trent sat perfectly still, his body drained, his heart twisted wreckage. *Damn her.* She'd made him do what he promised he wouldn't. He'd let her back in. His first instinct as he labored to breathe was to kiss her long and deep and never let her go. His second instinct was to remove her from his lap and kick her out of his office.

He did neither.

Instead, he sank his fingers into his hair, let his head fall back and stared at the ceiling. It was the pose of a man wondering what the hell he'd done.

Displaying no regret, Savannah pushed off the

couch and got to her feet. Hips swaying in unconscious allure, she crossed to the bar and found a towel, bringing it back to him. By the time Trent had cleaned up and disposed of the condom, she was putting the last hairpin into her impromptu updo. The only signs of how she'd spent the last ten minutes were her flushed cheeks and smeared lipstick.

He glanced up and down the length of her as she stepped back into her tall heels, and all he saw was a tranquil, confident woman. Gone was the femme fatale. Trent couldn't decide if he was glad or sorry.

"This doesn't change anything." His tone was brusque, his words more clipped than he'd intended. "I'm not going back to LA to bail out West Coast Records."

She looked at him askance, her eyebrows lifted in disbelief. "That's not what this was about."

"No?" But he knew she wasn't lying. Savannah frequently ended up in trouble because she wasn't calculating. The fact that he'd just accused her of unscrupulous behavior demonstrated that their unexpected sexual encounter had thrown him off his game. He hated that. It was time to take the situation back in his hands. "Where are you staying?"

His question surprised her. Something flickered in her eyes. "I'm not taking you to my hotel suite, if that's what you're thinking."

It wasn't what he'd been thinking, but now that she'd mentioned it, that sounded like a great idea. He'd like to strip that conservative dress off her and make love to her properly. But it was too late for that. Two years, one marriage and his brother's son too late.

"Where are you staying?" he repeated, letting her see that his patience was waning.

"Upstairs."

Cobalt had been Trent's first choice of location when he and his business partners decided to open Club T's. The hotel's owner, JT Stone, was a brilliant businessman with a great reputation and solid ethics. The rent was high for this exclusive real estate, but the hotel drew a chic crowd with deep pockets who liked to party and could easily afford Club T's high-end table service.

"I'll walk you back to your suite."

"There's no need."

Savannah wouldn't meet his eyes, and it was the first indication Trent had that the encounter had ruffled her composure.

"It's two in the morning." And Trent had no intention of returning to the club tonight. He'd lost his taste for partying the instant Savannah had appeared at his table. All he wanted was to head home, pour himself a liberal amount of scotch and brood. "And you've already had one run-in with a man you couldn't handle."

She gave an offhand shrug. "I think I handled you just fine."

He fought back an admiring smile. "I meant the guy in the bar."

"Oh, him." She shook her head. "I was on the verge of crushing his toe with my heel."

Unsure if she was kidding, Trent caught her by the elbow and turned her in the direction of the office door.

He led the way through the back halls of the club and hotel to a service elevator. Once inside he turned an expectant expression on her. Rather than tell him her floor, she reached to push the button herself.

"It's no good, you know," Trent said as the car began to move upward. "If you try to bring me in at West Coast Records, Siggy will fight you with everything he has."

"But you're exactly what the company needs. You're brilliant. Your father and Rafe never understood that."

Trent stared at her in bemusement. She'd always been on his side. How had two people who only had each other's best interest at heart failed so miserably at being together?

Because he didn't want what she did. Family for him meant nothing but heartache.

"You're wasting your time and mine. Let the company fold. You and Dylan will be fine without it. I'll make sure of that."

Three

Savannah turned Trent's words over and over in her mind as he escorted her to the suite. His offer made no sense.

At her door, she stopped and faced him. "You'll make sure how? I don't intend to take your money."

All she'd ever needed was for him to love her. She'd wanted to be his wife and raise his children. To make a secure life for her family and feel safe in turn. Being shipped between her father and grandmother for eight of her first eleven years had never allowed her any sense of belonging. That wasn't to say she didn't have good memories of the small town in Tennessee where her grandmother lived.

"You said you sold your house to pay Rafe's debts. Where are you going to go and what do you intend to live on?"

"I'd hoped to return to Tennessee." California was expensive and she wanted to start a new life far from the Caldwell family.

She never should have settled in LA after leaving New York. Originally she'd intended to move to Las Vegas to be close to Trent. He'd not been thrilled at having this plan sprung on him. It had been the first time she'd asserted herself and made her longing for marriage and a family clear to him. The fact that she'd pushed had caused their breakup. With her future up in the air, she'd gone to LA and reached out to Rafe.

He hadn't hit her with *I told you so* or made her feel worse about herself. He'd been supportive and friendly. A hundred times since then she'd wondered how her life would've turned out if she'd done any one of a dozen things differently.

"What's in Tennessee?" Trent asked.

Not a single thing, but at least it was somewhat familiar. "It's home."

He didn't look convinced. "And with no money, what are you planning on doing there?"

She'd considered returning to acting, but that would require relocating to New York or staying in LA. But with the terrifying load of debt hanging over her head, she was slowly coming around to the idea.

It meant giving up her dream of raising Dylan where neighbors knew each other and pitched in to help. At least for the time being.

"I had thought to move to Gatlinburg. The population is small, but it's a big tourist destination and I'm sure I can find something I can do."

"You didn't deserve to be put in this position by my family. You want to move to Tennessee, I'll help you with some cash to get you started."

She was okay with the idea of moving away, but Trent's offer of help made her feel as if he wanted her gone. Ridiculous. One brief sexual encounter with him and she was on her way to becoming emotionally attached again. *Damn.* This was not why she'd come here. She needed him to save the record label so Dylan would have something to inherit.

"The only help I need is for you to take over West Coast Records." Despair swept over her, but she couldn't let Trent see her distress. "Beyond that, there's nothing I need from you." She used her key card and let herself into the suite. "Good night, Trent. It was nice to see you again."

With a cheeky Courtney Day smile, she waved at him and slipped through the open doorway. She thought she'd gotten the final word in, but Trent had one last parting shot before the door closed.

"Take the night and think about my offer."

Savannah opened her mouth to tell him he was wasting his breath, but he'd already turned and walked away. She resisted the urge to call after him. She was tired of arguing.

With her plan to escape her current predicament amounting to a major failure, Savannah sought solace in the one spot of light. Her son, Dylan. She entered her bedroom, found him sleeping peacefully in his crib and turned off the baby monitor so as not to wake Lori, the babysitter Savannah had used on and off in the months since Rafe's death. Dylan was a sunny, healthy baby who'd begun sleeping through the night by the time he was six months old.

Having never known her mother, Savannah hadn't known what to expect when her son came along. Although she'd long craved a family of her own, reality was never the same as daydreams. In Dylan's case it was so much better.

Savannah left her sleeping son and crossed to the bathroom. She stripped off her dress and examined her bare thighs. Sure enough, a bruise was forming where Trent's fingers had bitten down. She brushed her fingertips across the spot. Letting her body dictate the encounter with Trent hadn't been the best idea, but she didn't regret what had happened. Yet she knew her impulsiveness would have emotional consequences.

Maybe she should take Trent's help to get out from under Rafe's load of debt. Let Siggy destroy the company. What did she care as long as she and Dylan were free? Besides, even if she could convince Trent to take on the leadership of the record label, she might be inviting more trouble from her father-in-law. He was leveraging her situation to keep Dylan close. What if he came after her with some ridiculous legal ploy that she couldn't afford to fight?

Savannah changed into pajamas but doubted her ability to sleep, so she turned on the television and sat on the couch in the living room to watch a show about tiny-house hunting. Her mood lightened somewhat as she considered the idea of finding a four-hundred-square-foot house where she and Dylan could live a simple life.

The sort of life she might have had with her mother if she hadn't been killed while deployed in the Middle East when Savannah had been three. She'd give anything to recall even the blurriest image of her mother, Libby. Instead, all she had were the stark memories of being passed back and forth between her father and maternal grandmother like an endless tennis volley.

Her parents had indulged in a brief fling that resulted in Savannah being conceived. And despite her resolve never to follow in her mother's footsteps, she'd done exactly that. From what she'd gathered from her grandmother, Libby hadn't planned to tell Chet Holt he was a father. Nor had Savannah's dad been thrilled to be saddled with the responsibility of a daughter he'd never expected.

When her father's bad decisions landed him in prison for burglary, and with her grandmother's health making it too hard for her to care for Savannah, she'd been shipped off to LA to live with her aunt, who worked as a housekeeper for the Caldwells.

Savannah closed her eyes and recalled the discomfort of her first few months in LA. The Caldwells' house was not a happy place. Siggy's second marriage was on the rocks, and Melody fought with her stepmother nonstop. At sixteen, Trent was raising hell at school and driving his father crazy at home. Only Rafe seemed above the fray. He'd been breezing through his senior year of high school and was on track to finish in the top 10 percent of his class.

With those unhappy days filling her thoughts, it was no wonder that when she fell asleep in front of the TV she had a nightmare about her and Dylan living in the Caldwell home with Siggy. She woke to the sounds of her son stirring in his bedroom and stumbled in a fog of lingering dismay to get him changed before Lori woke. Savannah loved these quiet early hours with Dylan.

Snuggling him enabled her to escape her worries for a little while. His smiles lit up a room. He was such a happy, inquisitive child and since he'd begun to walk two weeks ago, she had to keep a close eye on him at all times.

Both Savannah and Dylan were still in their pajamas when the babysitter emerged from her room. Savannah had given him breakfast and was on the couch reading to him from his favorite picture book.

"What time is it?" Savannah asked Lori, standing with Dylan in her arms.

"It's a little after eight."

"Why don't you order us some breakfast," Savannah said. "I'd like an egg-white omelet and toast."

The closing on her house was at two thirty that afternoon. Their flight back to LA was at eleven. Savannah handed over her son and headed to the bedroom to get ready. She didn't linger over her morning routine and had her bag packed in short order. By the time she emerged, a waiter was pushing a room service cart toward the large window that overlooked the Strip. Savannah signed for the breakfast, and the man headed for the door. When he opened it to leave, Trent was standing in the hall outside her suite.

"Good morning," he said, not waiting for an invitation to enter the room.

Trent's abrupt appearance threw her for a loop. She'd considered he might call. But never in her wildest dreams did she think he might actually show up in person this morning. Dressed in an impeccable navy superfine wool suit with a crisp white shirt and cobalt tie, Trent looked ready to do business.

Savannah shot a quick glance toward her son. He sat on the floor surrounded by books and toys, happily gnawing on a plastic key ring. Lori had seated herself at the dining room table and was removing the metal domes from the plates of food. She seemed uninterested in Savannah's visitor.

In the dark hours of late-night Vegas, reconnecting with her ex-lover had been relatively uncomplicated. In the cold light of day, with her son—Trent's son— less than ten feet away, she was feeling overwhelmed by her past mistakes and future missteps.

"What are you doing here?"

"You aren't really planning on moving to Tennessee, are you?"

After her troubled sleep and her dream about living in Siggy's house, Savannah was feeling less confident than she had been the night before. Despite what she'd told Trent, the truth was she had no place to go once she signed the papers on her house. She'd been so convinced she could get Trent to help her she hadn't focused at all on what would happen if she failed.

"I…" Her chest grew exceedingly tight. She couldn't get any words out.

"Are you okay?"

"Fine." The word had very little conviction behind it. Where was Courtney now? Savannah had lost her connection to her confident alter ego.

"Where are you planning to go, then?"

Misery engulfed her. "I don't have a plan." He'd never know what it cost her to admit that. Too many times he'd viewed her as helpless. "My only option was for you to help me with the company."

"But that doesn't help you with your immediate problem of where to go once you close on your house."

She knew he was right.

"I called Melody last night," Trent continued. "She's in Australia at the moment, and with the time difference it was afternoon. She told me Siggy wants you to move in with him. You're not planning on doing that, are you?"

Not if she could help it. Even as a temporary measure, becoming beholden to her father-in-law was a bad idea. Savannah exhaled in frustration but didn't respond to Trent's question. She couldn't blame Melody for telling Trent what was going on. Melody was just as upset as Savannah about the situation. Trent's sister had worked hard and suffered much to get out from beneath her father's weighty expectations.

"It's a bad idea."

"It's not what I want to do." She crossed her arms over her chest and stared past his shoulder. "I'd prefer to move to Tennessee and buy a small house there."

But was it really the place for her and Dylan? Savannah had latched on to Gatlinburg because her grandmother's house had been in a town twenty miles away, and she'd built it up in her mind as a great place to raise Dylan.

As if aware of her thoughts, Dylan gave a happy gurgle and stood. Trent's attention swiveled toward the toddler as Dylan began his ungainly waddle toward them.

"He's walking already?" Trent regarded the boy impassively. "I didn't think he was quite a year."

Savannah's pride shone through as she answered, "He's a little ahead of the curve." Seeing his mother's smile, Dylan came at her in a rush. With her heart thumping painfully hard, Savannah scooped him off the floor and settled him on her hip. He wrapped his hand around her three-tiered strand of pearls that complemented today's collared black sweater dress with three-quarter-length cuffed sleeves.

"Dylan, right?" Trent was inspecting the boy through narrowed eyes.

"Yes."

Father and son stared at each other while Savannah waited for what would happen next. She'd been dreading this encounter since the day her son had been born. Part of her hoped to see recognition in Trent's eyes. She wanted him to claim Dylan. Then she could stop feeling guilty for denying her son his father.

"You can't do this to him."

Savannah wasn't sure what she'd expected Trent to say, but that wasn't it. "Can't do what to him?"

"Let my father get his hands on him."

"You make it sound so ominous." She'd become

an expert at appearing more confident than she was. "What can Siggy do?"

"He could ruin his childhood the way he did Rafe's and mine."

From the expression on Savannah's face, she'd already considered this, and Trent's irritation grew. How could she even consider putting her son into such a toxic environment even for a few weeks? And then he realized her finances had to be in rough shape. What hadn't she told him?

"All right," he said, "let's stop dancing around."

Her eyes went round with apprehension. "What are you talking about?"

"I want to know exactly what's going on with you."

Savannah turned away and carried her son back to his toys. She then took her time pouring a cup of coffee and offering it to him. Trent shook his head.

"Dylan and I are returning to LA on an eleven o'clock flight. I have a closing on my house this afternoon. There's nothing else to tell."

Trent glanced around at the young woman working her way through a thick Belgian waffle and understood that Savannah would prefer not to air her business in front of the young woman.

"I was planning on heading to LA on business tomorrow. There's no reason why I couldn't go a day earlier. Perhaps you and I could celebrate after you close on your house and then tomorrow morning you could give me a tour of the company."

Savannah grimaced. "I'm not sure closing on my house is a reason to celebrate."

"Then just consider it an opportunity for the two of us to get reacquainted."

"Do you really want a tour of the company?" She sounded uncertain.

He hoped she was worried about how his father would react to her bringing Trent into West Coast Records. Her notion that he could do something to help her save the company was crazy.

"Absolutely. Why don't you give Gerry a call and tell him you're bringing by your financial adviser to look over the books."

Savannah gave him the first genuine smile he'd seen. "He's not going to be happy about that."

"Do you really care?"

"Siggy isn't going to be happy about that, either." It didn't appear as if that bothered her, but Trent suspected it did a little. His father was bound to make her life miserable if he discovered she'd teamed up with Trent. "Are you going to help me with the company?"

"No." His intention was simply to let his father think that's what he intended to do. Perhaps then Siggy would buy back his company from Savannah, allowing her and Dylan to head off to her new life in Tennessee.

She looked confused by his answer. "Then why do you want to see the books?"

"Something has to be going on," he said. Overnight his curiosity had been aroused by what she had told him. While he'd heard West Coast Records was struggling, things didn't sound as if they were bad enough for them to stop paying their artists. "It doesn't surprise me that profits are down, but something more serious must be happening if things are in the state you say they are."

"What if Gerry refuses to give me the information?"

"Then we'll have our answer as to who is at the center of what's going on there, won't we?"

"You think Gerry has something to do with this?"

"With Siggy retired and Rafe sick, he was in the perfect position to mismanage the company." And Trent had never been particularly impressed with the man's business savvy. "So let's go see what's going on, shall we? I've chartered a plane. I'll pick you up downstairs at ten thirty."

"We're already scheduled on a flight to LA."

"It will be easier if I'm not chasing all over LAX looking for you." He softened his tone. "And it will be more comfortable for you."

Trent felt a tug on his pant leg and looked down. His nephew was standing, looking up at him. The boy's blue eyes, so reminiscent of Rafe's, were fixed on Trent's face. Something in his chest tightened. All at once he couldn't breathe.

This was Rafe's son. Savannah's son. Like a man drowning, Trent saw his past with Savannah flash before his eyes. The joy on that Christmas morning when she'd woken up to Murphy's sweet puppy face and adorable snuffles. What had he been thinking? He'd bought her a dog. She'd been feeling gloomy about spending the holidays alone. So he bought her something to take care of and flown to New York to give it to her. Making a woman happy had never been as easy as it had been with her.

And then because she'd misinterpreted his gift, he'd felt compelled to distance himself for months after.

When the toddler continued to stare at Trent, he bent down and picked the boy up. He didn't have much experience with children, but something about his nephew made it a simple thing to settle the child against his chest as if he'd done it a hundred times before. The amount of curiosity in the infant's eyes intrigued Trent. What could possibly be going on in that developing brain of his?

Dylan latched on to Trent's tie the same way he'd grabbed Savannah's pearls, and Trent heard her soft cry of dismay.

"He's going to ruin your tie," she said, stepping toward them with her hands outstretched as if to take her son.

"It's just a tie." Trent pivoted away from her advance. He couldn't explain his sudden reluctance to give the child up. "It looks like your breakfast is getting cold. Why don't you sit down and eat? Dylan and I will be just fine."

The distress in Savannah's eyes made no sense. It wasn't as if he was going to spirit the infant out of the suite. He had no interest in his nephew outside of satisfying a brief bit of curiosity about him.

Rafe had died within months of his son being born. Having a father like Siggy, Trent had little positive experience when it came to father-son bonding. Would Dylan suffer never knowing his dad? On the other hand, once Savannah settled in Tennessee, she might marry again and Dylan would be raised by a stepfather. Either way, at least he would grow up dearly loved by his mother. That much was clear.

Trent picked up one of the picture books from the floor near Dylan's toys and sat down on the couch with the boy.

"That's his favorite," Savannah said, sitting with an untouched plate of eggs before her. "He'd love it if you read it to him."

Left on his own with the boy, Trent opened the book and began reading while Dylan patted the pages with his fat little hands and wiggled. Trent found himself smiling. For the last year he'd avoided thinking about his nephew. Although he'd never intended to saddle himself with a wife and children, the fact that Savannah had given his brother a son ate at him.

Rafe had gotten everything. Their father's love and approval. The family business. And Savannah. The first two Trent had come to terms with. The last one had blasted a hole in his heart big enough to drive a semi through. But it was his own fault. He could've had her. Dylan could have been his son. Except the conventional family Savannah craved wasn't what he wanted.

The idea that anyone would rely on him was a suffocating weight. Sure, he'd helped her out several times in the past, but those had been random acts when it had been convenient for him. He had to do things on his terms, not on anyone else's. Even now, stepping up to help her with the label, he wasn't doing it for her. He was doing it to piss off his old man.

Trent wanted to see if Siggy hated him enough to bankrupt the record label before he would let his son be in charge. To Trent's recollection, his father had never shown him anything but disdain. Rafe had been the favorite son. Siggy's firstborn. He'd taken after his father in appearance and mind-set: a businessman mired in ego and lacking vision.

Like his sister, Melody, Trent had inherited his mother's voice and musical talent. Not that he had any interest in pursuing a career in the business. He left the songwriting, piano playing and singing to his younger sister. Trent could not be more proud of Melody.

She'd struggled to find her wings in a household that didn't appreciate what she could do. Forced to attend Juilliard as a classic violinist when what she really wanted to do was compose pop songs for others to perform, Melody had dropped out of school midway through her junior year of college.

The gap in their ages had kept Trent from knowing Melody as well as he could. But when he'd gone to visit her in New York City and she'd come clean about her passion for writing music, he'd been behind her 100 percent about quitting school. She needed money to rent studio time to make a demo of her music and he'd happily provided it. He'd also put her in contact with the people in the music industry who could help her get started.

This bit of assistance and support had only added to the acrimony between Trent and his father. It was shortly after this that Siggy stopped speaking with Trent. The owner of West Coast Records had a vision in his head regarding his daughter, and it had nothing to do with her lowering herself to being someone else's songwriter.

Trent hadn't understood his father's perspective. Melody was immensely talented. She could have become an incredible star if she'd been interested in the spotlight. But she preferred being behind the scenes and having her music developed by others. At least that's the way it'd been until his friend and partner in Club T's, Nate Tucker, had convinced her to bring her violin on tour with Free Fall. Seeing a star in the making, Tucker had pushed her to sing one of her songs during his set. It had gone so well that she was now opening for him.

And as far as Siggy was concerned, this was Trent's fault, too.

"How are things going?"

Trent looked up from the book and spied Savannah standing before him. Although her makeup was flawless, he thought she looked pale. Was that brought on by stress or lack of sleep? He'd had a hard time settling down after walking her to her suite. Although he was no stranger to spontaneous encounters, usually the moments lingered in his mind for a short time and then faded away.

With Savannah everything was different.

He couldn't just revel in a quickie with his brother's widow, chuckle at the irony and move on. There was too much history between them. Too much he couldn't stop himself from needing.

"Great," he said. "You're right about him liking this book."

"He enjoys being read to." She smiled fondly at her son. "I guess what kid doesn't."

"I don't remember anyone reading to me, do you?"

Savannah shook her head. "My grandmother used to tell me stories about when she was a little girl. She grew up on a farm in Kansas and talked about milking the cows and barn cats having kittens. She described what it had been like to be in the cellar while a tornado took out the chicken coop but missed the barn and house."

Her distant gaze and fond smile clashed with Trent's attitude about his own upbringing. His childhood memories mainly consisted of watching TV and playing video games. His mother had never read to him. She'd been busy maintaining her appearance and chasing her own happiness. Personal trainers, self-help quacks and an assortment of assistants had kept Trent's mother lean of body and calm of spirit. Or at least they had tried to. Living with someone as critical as Siggy Caldwell was debilitating for anyone without sufficient self-esteem.

These days Naomi was a very different person. She laughed all the time and allowed herself to age gracefully. After leaving Siggy, she'd moved to New York and gotten some off-Broadway work. It was there she'd met and married her second husband, investment banker Larry Fry.

"I'm going to get Dylan ready to leave."

"I have to check out a couple things at the club before I go."

Trent gave up the boy, surprised at his reluctance to do so. Despite the fact that Dylan was a baby, he'd enjoyed the child's company more than he'd expected. But there was a huge difference between playing the part of fun uncle who spent ten minutes reading a book and a lifetime of caretaking as a father.

Savannah settled her son on her hip and spoke in a light voice. "Dylan, can you wave goodbye to your uncle Trent?"

The nearly one-year-old child did as he was bidden and followed it up by blowing a kiss. Trent was impressed by the boy's tricks and wondered if this was average for kids his age.

He didn't want to like his nephew any more than he wanted to get embroiled in Savannah's problems. But something was going on with West Coast Records, and his curiosity wouldn't let him turn it aside.

Besides, there might be an opportunity here and he'd be a fool to pass that up.

Four

While Trent negotiated the LA traffic, Savannah sat like a stone beside him. As of twenty minutes ago, she was officially homeless. Sunshine poured through the car window, but Savannah enjoyed neither the soothing brightness nor the warmth.

"Are you okay?" Trent had been casting glances her way since he'd picked her up from the closing.

"Dylan and I have nowhere to go." Her vision blurred as her eyes filled with unshed tears. She blinked them away. What was wrong with her that she stumbled from one desperate situation to another? "I'm a complete failure as a mother."

"Don't say things like that."

"I haven't done a good job providing for him or protecting him."

"This isn't a problem you created."

While she appreciated Trent's attempt to make her feel better, she couldn't ignore the string of bad decisions that had led her to this place. On the other hand, one of her choices, foolish or not, had given her the light of her life, her son.

"Maybe not a problem I created, but when I discovered how bad things were financially, I should have gone back to work and found us a place to live." She dug her fingernails into her hands to keep a grip on her anxiety. "Instead I stuck my head in the sand."

"Stop being so hard on yourself."

"Tell me you would've acted the same and I won't say another word."

"We don't come at problems the same way."

"Ha." To her surprise, arguing with Trent was making her feel better. She might be down, but she certainly didn't have to be out. "What do you think we're going to find at the label?"

Trent's expression darkened. "This is probably the wrong thing to say to you right now, but you probably should brace yourself for some unpleasantness."

"Too late," she said. "I called Gerry this morning before leaving the hotel, and he was not pleased by my request. So I'm completely convinced we will have a fight on our hands."

"Did you tell him I was coming?"

Savannah smiled. "And lose the element of surprise?"

Ten minutes later, Trent entered West Coast Records' parking lot and pulled into a visitor's spot. She put her hand on his arm as he made to open his door.

"Thank you," she said, seeing Siggy's car parked in Rafe's spot. "I know coming here isn't easy for you."

"It doesn't bother me."

From his expression, she couldn't tell whether or not that was true. She indicated her father-in-law's car. "Have you spoken to Siggy since Rafe's funeral?"

"No. We have nothing to say to each other."

To Savannah's relief, there'd been no father-son blowup at Rafe's funeral. The two Caldwell men had stood apart from each other the entire day and never indulged the ongoing animosity between them. She might not have loved Rafe, but Savannah had wanted his family and friends to mourn him uninterrupted by squabbling.

As much as Savannah longed to take strength from Trent's solid presence at her side, she kept her chin up and a respectable distance between them as they entered the building and strode across the bright, open lobby. West Coast Records had been located here since the '50s. Siggy had bought the company in 1976.

It had done well for a lot of years, but with the shift into digital, the label had been too slow to evolve and hadn't developed a solid plan of action to make money in the age when people didn't have to download an entire album but could pick and choose which songs they wanted.

From what Savannah had come to understand from her own research and what Trent had explained during the flight, West Coast Records had signed a bunch of artists and flooded the marketplace with mediocre music. They were trying to re-create the huge revenues they used to enjoy instead of spending the time it took to develop real talent and accepting that they were going to make smaller amounts than they used to.

Savannah led the way past the unoccupied reception desk toward Rafe's office. She hadn't been here more than a half-dozen times, but she knew the way well enough. As they moved through the halls, she noticed an abundance of empty desks. The whole building had a stillness to it that made her uncomfortable. At four in the afternoon, it was possible that the staff had gone for the day, but the lack of personal items at the desks made the office feel like a ghost town.

"Where is everyone?" she asked Trent, slowing down to peer around her. "It looks deserted."

"Maybe they've laid off some people."

The anxiety that had plagued her for months increased. What if she'd brought Trent in too late? If the company failed, the stock would be worthless. Right now she was using a small income she received from the company to pay the minimum on the debt until she could figure something out. If the label failed, that would dry up. Then, her only recourse would be to declare bankruptcy to get out from beneath Rafe's massive debt.

On the way to Rafe's office, they passed Gerry's.

"Any idea where Gerry is hiding?" Trent asked, arching one eyebrow. His reaction to being here was the polar opposite of hers. The worse things appeared, the more relaxed he became.

"I haven't been here since I found out Rafe was sick. Maybe Gerry took over Rafe's office."

When they entered the president's office, they found not only Gerry, but also Siggy. The old man was seated behind the desk as if he was still in charge. At the sight of him in her dead husband's executive chair, Savannah's anxiety became annoyance.

"What are you doing here?" Sigmund Caldwell demanded, getting to his feet in an explosive movement. Palms planted on the desk, he scowled at his younger son.

"Hello, Siggy." Trent took a step past Savannah, positioning himself like a protective guard dog. "I'm surprised to find you in the office." Thanks to the amusement in his tone, he didn't sound surprised.

"Trent is here because I asked him to come." Savannah held her expression neutral as her father-in-law's sharp gaze shifted to her. "I need to know what's going on with the company's financials."

"You don't need to know anything," Siggy said.

"That isn't true. With Rafe's death Dylan inherits his shares, and I'm his mother. It falls to me to make sure his inheritance survives." Savannah knew immediately she'd gone too far.

"Nothing falls to you. You are just a grasping woman who took advantage of my son's illness. If you think I'm going to let you make decisions about this company, you are sadly mistaken."

"Fine. Then buy the shares back." She was shaking, but the confrontation with her father-in-law was not as bad as it would have been without Trent at her side. She could never have done this without him.

Siggy looked her over, his disdain apparent. "I have a better idea. Why don't I pay you to go away? You leave the boy with me, and I set you up somewhere far away."

It was the deal he'd made with his first wife, Naomi Caldwell. "I have no intention of giving you my son."

The way Siggy smiled broadcast his skepticism. And given his ability to manipulate both his former wives, that didn't really surprise her.

"As you said, this company will belong to my grandson one day. The shares are his. I will manage it until he is ready to take over."

"But you are no longer the managing partner, nor are you the majority shareholder," Trent pointed out in a reasonable voice.

The instant he spoke, his father's attention swung back to him once more. "You do not belong here. If you don't leave now, I'll have security throw you out."

"Security? Word on the street is you can't afford security anymore."

Siggy's face grew ruddy. "Get out," he spat.

"Not without the financials," Trent retorted. He was as calm as his father was upset. "As guardian of the majority shareholder, Savannah needs to see what's going on."

Observing the exchange between father and son, Savannah almost felt sorry for her father-in-law. If Siggy hadn't been such a domineering bastard, perhaps they could've work through their differences amicably. But

Siggy wanted to maintain control of his company, and to do so he needed control over her son.

With the four of them staring each other down, Savannah wasn't sure what would happen next. Without access to the computers, she had no idea how they could force Gerry or Siggy to open up the books.

But apparently, Trent knew exactly what he was doing. "Things will not go well for you if we get lawyers involved," he said ominously.

As a privately held company, West Coast Records was not required to file any public documents regarding its finances. The board membership was composed of six of Siggy's cronies but Savannah doubted they would be interested in being on the receiving end of any legal action she might take against them on behalf of her son.

"Gerry, give them access." Siggy slid from behind the desk, stalked up to his son and glared at him. "You might have won this round but I'll burn West Coast Records to the ground before I'll let you anywhere near this company."

Bold words, Savannah thought. But as she watched her father-in-law exit the room, she wasn't completely sure if it was bravado or a touch of madness that drove him where Trent was concerned.

Gerry did something with the computer and then left the room, as well.

As Trent slid behind the desk and began tapping away, Savannah sank into a guest chair opposite him.

"How do you do it?" She sat with her hands clasped

tight in her lap and exhaled to calm herself. "How do you face him down so calmly? Doesn't he get to you?"

"Years of practice have taught me to cope." But stress lines had appeared beside his compressed lips and his eyes were guarded.

Long minutes ticked by while Trent looked through the computer records. Savannah had a hard time containing her restless energy. Any second she expected Siggy to reappear and begin to berate her once more. If before this she'd been determined to keep Dylan out of his clutches, now she was even more convinced she couldn't let her son be anywhere near him.

She paced around the room, paying special attention to the photos and awards that lined the walls. From the look of things, the label hadn't had any great success since the early '90s. And she had a hard time finding Rafe's stamp on anything. This made her sad. In many ways her husband had been trapped by his position as eldest son.

Could he have done as Trent had and made his own way? Savannah wasn't sure Rafe had it in him to break free of his father's hold. Rafe was firstborn. His father's pride and joy. The weight of expectation had turned him into a mini Siggy.

"Finding anything?" She came to stand behind Trent and peer over his shoulder at the monitor.

Despite the seriousness of her situation, the stressful confrontation with Siggy and her fears for her son, she couldn't stop herself from snatching a lungful of Trent's familiar cologne. Her head spun as her senses came alive. His long fingers darted across the keyboard and she couldn't help herself from remembering how they'd felt biting down on her skin as she came the previous night.

His thick, wavy hair enticed a woman's fingers to roam. Not a speck of lint dotted the shoulders of his dark blue suit, but that didn't stop Savannah's craving to sweep her fingers across the material. Last night's reckless encounter had stirred up a beehive of longing. She hungered to touch him again and was willing to make up lame excuses to do so. Before she succumbed to temptation, she put her hands behind her back.

"What are you doing? That doesn't look like financial records."

At her question, Trent didn't glance up. "A friend of mine lent me a program." He removed a flash drive from the computer's USB port and slipped it into his pocket.

"What sort of program?" Savannah stepped back as he got to his feet.

"I'll tell you in the car."

"Is all this really necessary?" She wasn't sure what to make of Trent's cloak-and-dagger routine. Was he behaving this way for her benefit? Acting as if the trip to West Coast Records' offices was more productive than it had been?

Trent spread his fingers across the small of her back and nudged her toward the hallway. "Let's go."

Obviously he wasn't going to say another word while they were still in the building. As badly as she wanted to know what was going on, Savannah was enjoying the warmth of his palm far too much to be hurried.

As on the way in, they encountered no one, but the boardroom door was closed as they passed. Once in the parking lot, Savannah couldn't restrain her curiosity one second longer. "What's going on? Were you able to determine anything from the financials?"

"They gave us only the most rudimentary access."

"What does that mean?"

"That means they were ready for us. We got a year-to-date profit and loss statement and balance sheet. It shows that the company is profitable."

"How profitable?"

"Enough that they should be paying their artists. But you say they aren't."

"That's the impression that I was given. Maybe they are paying some but not all."

"Money is going out," Trent said, opening the passenger door so she could slide in. "I just can't determine if it's actually going to the artists." Without saying another word, he shut the car door, leaving her to mull over his last statement.

She waited until he'd slid behind the wheel and started the engine before repeating her earlier question. "What was with the USB drive?"

"I figured we wouldn't get much. So I came prepared. A friend of mine in Vegas runs a security company. And he wouldn't want it spread around, but he's a gifted hacker. I called him this morning, explained the problem, and he gave me a worm to implant in their system."

"A worm?" Savannah had watched enough TV to know what he was talking about. But she had never considered that real people used them. "Are you telling me you planted some sort of spy software in the company's computer system?"

"As good a hacker as he is, he could've cracked their system from the outside, but why bother when it's so much easier to do it from the inside?"

Savannah was starting to feel hopeful. "So what does this get us?"

"Full access to their system."

Leave it to Trent to come to her rescue once again. Savannah would never have conceived of something so clever and potentially illegal.

"So you'll be able to see what's actually going on?"

"That's the idea."

"Is it illegal?"

"I'd say it's a gray area. Dylan is the majority shareholder in the company. They are denying you access to the books." Trent backed the car out of the parking spot. "But it doesn't matter. Logan assures me his software's untraceable. They'll never know what hit them."

Adrenaline buzzed through Trent's veins as he negotiated the LA traffic on the way to the hotel Savannah had chosen until she found a more permanent place to settle. The fight with his father had gone as expected. Trent glanced at Savannah. She hadn't reacted well to Siggy's vicious attack. It had taken a great deal of willpower to keep from acknowledging her distress and comforting her back at the label. He didn't want either her or his father to get the idea something was going on between them.

In the old days when he and his father had fought, she had often come to him with comforting words. Initially he'd rebuffed her attempts to make him feel better, not understanding what she needed was reassurance that he was all right.

He glanced at her now. She stared out the passenger window. Her face was impassive, but her hands, clasped around the purse in her lap, were rigid with tension. He recognized that she was stressed. He gathered breath, refrained from speaking. What was he going to say? That everything was going to be fine? He didn't know that. And what was he doing getting more deeply involved in her problem with his father when he'd determined a decade earlier that he was done with the family drama?

"Dealing with Siggy isn't going to be fun or easy," he said, stating the obvious. "Are you sure you don't want me to help you get back on your feet somewhere besides here?"

When he made the offer the night before, he hadn't done so as an ex-lover or a brother-in-law. They'd been friends long before either of those things, and whether he'd always been able to admit it or not, she'd been there for him during some very dark days.

"I told you last night that I'm not going to take your money."

"You could think of it as a loan."

Her features relaxed into a wry expression. "I've

considered that," she explained in an overly patient tone. "My answer is still no."

When had she become stubborn? Trent caught himself frowning. She wasn't the same woman he'd broken up with two years earlier. And he wasn't sure what to make of the change.

"Why are you so opposed to letting me help you?"

"I wouldn't be in the car with you if I was opposed to letting you help me."

"Then why won't you take money from me? It's not as if I'd notice it was gone."

She cocked her head and stared straight forward. "I can't explain it. Getting you to help me sort out what's wrong at West Coast Records isn't personal. I could hire a lawyer to do that."

"I thought you were broke?"

"I might be able to afford a really bad attorney," she retorted with a trace of a smile. And then she sighed. "To be honest, I wasn't thinking straight before last night."

"Last night? What changed last night?"

"Have you forgotten already?" Her voice packed just the right amount of sultry amusement to stir his lust.

He tightened his grip on the steering wheel to keep his hands from wandering across the space between them and slipping beneath the hem of her dress to find her bare knee. It drove him crazy that ever since she'd been married his brother she'd started dressing to repress her sensuality. A beautiful woman shouldn't hide the way Savannah did.

"Hardly." But after glancing in her direction, he

wasn't sure if they were referring to the same thing after all. "You are talking about what happened in my office, aren't you?"

"You sound worried that I'm not."

"I don't sound worried." What was going on that he wanted last night's encounter to have changed her somehow?

It had been an interlude between ex-lovers. Nothing more. It certainly hadn't changed anything going on with him. So why did he expect her to be any different? Trent ground his teeth together, disliking his uncertainty. To his relief, Savannah chose to elaborate without his prompting.

"Being around you reminded me of the girl I used to be. You taught me how to take care of myself. I'd forgotten how to do that in the last year and a half."

As long as he could remember, he'd lectured her on the need to question people's motives before agreeing to something. She'd lost much of her naïveté while living in New York, but obviously she sometimes forgot to be wary of people eager to take advantage of her.

"Why didn't you take care of yourself while married to my brother?"

"In a lot of ways, your brother was like your father. He wanted a particular kind of wife. One who did as he asked and never argued. I didn't realize our marriage wasn't going to be a partnership until too late."

For the first time, it occurred to Trent that she hadn't been happy. Again came that urge to comfort her. Again he resisted. She wasn't his to worry about. Helping her sort through what was going on with the label was about getting back at his father. She'd hit the nail on the head last night when she'd encouraged him to demonstrate to Siggy that he was a better businessman.

"I'm sorry things didn't work out the way you'd hoped."

"I'm not sure I had an idea what I was hoping for."

Again her remark prompted questions, but Trent refrained from diving in. Last night she'd said she didn't want to talk about her marriage. He sure as hell didn't want to hear about it today.

He parked the car in the hotel parking lot and they went in the front entrance together. She'd chosen a budget chain, with none of the bells and whistles she might have enjoyed if his brother hadn't left her in debt. Whatever else had changed with her, she remained fiscally responsible.

Trent had booked himself into the Wilshire for the night. Although he could very easily have dropped Savannah off and headed to his hotel, he felt as if he owed her some idea of what he had planned.

Her standard hotel room was empty when they arrived. A crib had been set up by the window, but Dylan wasn't in it and the babysitter was nowhere to be seen.

"Shouldn't they be here?" For some reason the sight of the empty hotel room alarmed him. Maybe it was the way Savannah had tensed.

"I told Lori not to go anywhere until I got back." Savannah fumbled in her purse for her phone and scrolled through her contacts. "She didn't send me a text and she's not answering her phone. Where could they be?" The pitch of her voice registered anxiety.

"How long have you known this girl?"

"I first hired her to babysit Dylan right after Rafe's death. I knew there would be a lot to do and that it would disrupt Dylan's routines too much if I brought him everywhere I needed to go."

"And you checked her out?"

Savannah shot him a dark look. "I hired her through a reputable agency that had her thoroughly vetted."

"And she hasn't done anything like this before?"

"If by *like this* you mean taken Dylan somewhere without telling me, not to my knowledge."

Trent could tell his interrogation of Savannah wasn't helping the situation, and she was looking more upset by the minute.

"What is it you aren't telling me?" Trent demanded.

"Nothing really."

"I don't believe you."

"It's just that your father…"

Savannah had been dialing as she'd begun her explanation. Now she spoke to the person who'd answered. "Aunt Stacy," Savannah said into the phone. "I was wondering if Lori is still there with Dylan?" She paused and her entire body slumped with relief. "No, that's fine. I wasn't expecting him to be gone. Lori didn't say anything about heading over there." A pause. "Oh, he did? No, he didn't say anything to me about it."

Fury rose in Trent while he waited for her to finish chatting with her aunt. The part of him that wasn't plotting his father's downfall admired Savannah's ability to remain calm and think under pressure.

"No need to mention I called," Savannah was saying, her voice showing no stress at all. "I'll be by in a bit."

When she disconnected the call, she sank onto the bed and put her face in her hands. Her body shook as she gasped in a ragged breath. Trent put his hand on her shoulder. She jerked away as if burned. Her blue eyes were hot as she gazed up into his face. But as quickly as her temper flared, she calmed down.

"Sorry. That wasn't directed at you." She waved her hand in a random gesture. "Lori took Dylan over to Siggy's."

"Without saying anything to you or asking if it was okay?"

"He told her he'd cleared it with me." She rose, her movements stiff and slow as if every muscle in her body ached. "I guess I messed with him so he messed with me."

"I should have anticipated something like this."

"Neither of us had any way of knowing." Her neutral tone was at odds with the fear and anger she'd demonstrated moments earlier. "I'm sorry to ask for another favor, but do you mind driving me over there? It looks as if Lori helped herself to my car."

"Whatever you need."

Five minutes later, they were back in the LA traffic. Savannah's fierce demeanor invited no conversation. Trent kept his focus on the road. The drive to his father's house took over an hour. It was a tense sixty minutes. He couldn't imagine what she was going through, the panic she must have felt coming back to the hotel and finding her son gone, the roller coaster of emotions when she figured out the nanny had taken Dylan to his grandfather.

Trent wanted to be there when she faced down Siggy, but when they pulled up to the enormous Beverly Hills mansion, she shook her head when he shut off the car.

"I need to do this on my own."

"Are you sure that's your best option? My father will try to bully you."

"He's gone too far this time."

"Call me when you're on your way back to the hotel." Everything in him was clamoring to accompany her into the mansion and act as her champion. "I need to know you're okay."

"I'm going to be just fine."

"Regardless. Call me."

With a nod, Savannah got out of the car and Trent stared at the mansion's front door long after she was lost from view.

Five

Savannah's heels clicked against the travertine tile of the wide entryway as she let herself into Siggy's mansion. The earlier heat of anger had been replaced by icy determination. Ever since she'd come to live in this house at age eleven, she'd been intimidated by the man who lived here. She'd seen how he criticized his sons, dominated his staff and intimidated his business associates.

But today he'd stopped being someone to fear. Today, he'd interfered with her son, and she would do whatever it took to make sure that never happened again.

Set on a half-acre lot, the modern house had a wide-open floor plan that was perfect for entertaining. As a child, Savannah had witnessed hundreds of parties, and when she was old enough, she'd served at many.

The backyard had enough space for a large pool with a broad black-and-white marble surround, a pool house and a separate outdoor dining area for twelve beside an expansive fire feature.

Although the house was fifteen thousand square feet, there were only six bedrooms, and the way the public spaces opened onto each other, it was easy for her to find Siggy and Dylan in the main living room.

Lori was the first one to catch sight of her. Siggy was on the phone near the middle set of French doors that opened onto the backyard, his back to her. Dylan toddled along the espresso-toned hardwood floors that flowed into the dining room. Savannah made straight for him and snatched him into her arms. Pausing for a brief second to hug him and breathe in his familiar scent, she then turned to her babysitter.

"Give me my car keys and get out of here before I have you arrested."

The girl backed away from Savannah's advance, obviously terrified. "I didn't do anything wrong," she protested. "He asked me to come by with the baby. He said it was okay. He told me you knew."

"I don't care what he said. I hired you. You only answer to me." Savannah felt no remorse at scaring the girl after what she'd done. She put her hand out and stared daggers at Lori until she put the car keys in Savannah's palm.

"How am I supposed to get home?"

"I couldn't care less."

Savannah turned her back on the girl and headed for the foyer. While a part of her wanted to confront Siggy, she knew she would lose the battle. However, before she could reach the foyer, a tall broad-shouldered man in a black suit stepped in her path.

"I can't let you leave."

A little dazed by what he'd just said, Savannah was momentarily stumped for a response. Was she to be a prisoner? Savannah considered the surge of independence with which she'd turned down Trent's offer of support. Never in a million years had she thought Siggy would prevent her from leaving.

First she scowled at the man blocking her way, but seeing he had no intention of moving, she glanced over her shoulder at her father-in-law. He was still on the phone and didn't acknowledge the standoff happening twenty feet away. The righteous fury that had carried her this far had started to subside, but mounting panic gave her an adrenaline boost. She'd prepared herself to reclaim her son and fire Lori. She hadn't planned on having to save herself, as well.

"Step aside," she told the man and silently cursed when she heard the slight tremor in her voice. The entranceway he blocked was ten feet wide, leaving plenty of room to go around him, but with Dylan in her arms and four-inch heels on her feet, she doubted she could move fast enough on the marble floor to make a break for it.

"I can't let you go until he says it's okay."

Unwilling to argue with the man further, Savannah turned her back on Siggy. Frustration and helplessness washed over her. She hated feeling this way. It was how she'd felt from the moment she'd slid Rafe's ring onto her finger. Why had she let him talk her into marrying him? She should have toughened up and trusted she could handle being a single mom.

Siggy concluded his call and headed in her direction. Savannah barely let him take three steps before venting her outrage.

"How dare you try to keep us here." She didn't care if this was the wrong tack to take with her father-in-law. "Call off your gorilla. Dylan and I are leaving now."

"We need to talk."

"There is nothing to talk about. Dylan and I are leaving."

"To go where?" He might have sounded reasonable, but his eyes flashed with disdain. "You have no money and you are deep in debt."

"Thanks to your son."

"He was sick."

"Yes, and he made a lot of bad choices. It left me with a huge financial burden and barely anything for Dylan and me to live on. You know he would hate that."

"I know that he would like for me to take care of his son."

His son. But not her. Instinctively, Savannah tightened her hold on Dylan and shifted so that her body was between her son and the two men who flanked her. Would they try to take him by force? Savannah pushed down dismay. She would not leave here without her Dylan, but couldn't bear the thought of staying. They would be prisoners.

"Then please buy back the stock Rafe left Dylan. Give us the chance for a fresh start."

"A fresh start? What sort of fresh start are you looking for?"

"I thought I would find a small house for just the two of us, and go back to work."

"You mean acting." He said it with a great deal of derision. "That wouldn't be necessary if you moved in here."

Around and around the argument went. She and Siggy had been wearing out this topic since shortly after Rafe's death nine months ago.

"I want Dylan to live in a neighborhood filled with children who come over after school to play."

She had this idyllic image in her head of small-town living, where her house was the most popular one on the block with the kids. Siggy's Hollywood home was a showplace and not one bit kid friendly.

"He's not old enough to go to school."

And by the time he was, she'd be well and firmly trapped. "Do you plan on keeping me here by force?"

"Of course not. You're free to go whenever you wish."

"Thank you." She turned to go, but her way was still blocked. "I wish to go now."

From behind her came Siggy's smooth voice. "Dylan stays."

Savannah fought down panic. "We're both leaving."

For a span of several heartbeats, no one moved. Then the front door opened and Trent stepped inside.

Trent left the front door open as he crossed the expansive foyer. The man barring Savannah's path had two inches and thirty pounds on Trent, but he didn't see this as a problem.

He looked into Savannah's eyes and hoped she'd follow his lead. "We have a plane to catch. And you know how the traffic is."

"Yes, of course." Her gaze searched his.

"She's not going anywhere." Siggy actually appeared to think he could get away with compelling Savannah to stay by bullying her.

"That's not true," Savannah stated, her relief obvious. She took the hand Trent held out to her and came to stand beside him. "Dylan and I were trying to leave, but your father was threatening me."

"Is that true?"

Siggy didn't answer Trent's question but instead asked one of his own. "So you're cheating on your husband with him?"

"Rafe is dead. She can't cheat on his memory."

"And it's no business of yours who I'm with." Savannah shook her head. "Trent is family and he's helping me. Something you should be doing."

"Neither one of you is going to get anywhere near the company again."

"Dylan owns a majority share. That means I'm in control until he turns twenty-one. You have nothing to say about it."

"It's my company. I built it. I have everything to say about it."

"Not unless you buy the shares back."

"I don't have to buy the shares back," Siggy said,

his eyes burning with malice. "All I need is control of my grandson."

Beside him, Savannah stiffened. Trent stepped forward. "Do not threaten her."

Siggy sneered. "Or what?"

Trent wasn't a reckless teenager anymore, but his father continued to treat him with contempt. Since striking out to make it on his own, Trent was less and less bothered by his father's low opinion. He'd come to accept that no matter how successful he was, nothing diminished Siggy's disapproval.

"Try me and see." Trent gave his father a cold smile, set his hand on Savannah's back and guided her toward the front door.

She was trembling as they crossed from the cold foyer into the bright afternoon sunshine, but as they headed across the driveway to her car, she released a shaky smile.

"I've never been so happy to see anybody in my entire life."

"That's probably not something you would've said yesterday."

She opened her car's back door and settled Dylan into his seat. "You might be surprised."

Trent waited for her to say more, but she simply buckled her son in and closed the door. At last she faced him, and her gorgeous smile hit him like a two-by-four. Unfortunately it was gone as fast as it had arrived.

"I don't have to tell you how frightening that was. He wants to take Dylan away from me."

"You need to contact a lawyer and get ahead of this."

"You're right." Her shoulders slumped. "But right now I need to get out of here."

While Trent followed her back to her hotel, a plan began to form in his mind. He parked next to her in the hotel's large lot and intercepted her as she was getting out of her car.

"You can't stay here."

She didn't look happy as she gazed toward the hotel's shabby facade. "But it's only temporary."

The longer he was with Savannah, the more he felt driven to fix things for her. It was an old pattern. One he thought he'd abandoned when she'd married Rafe. "I don't mean the hotel. I mean LA."

"I don't want to, but with everything that's going on with the company, I can't leave until things are settled." She wasn't acknowledging how dire her situation was. Alone in LA, she would be at Siggy's mercy.

"You and Dylan are coming back to Las Vegas with me."

Trent didn't second-guess his decision to get further entangled with Savannah and her son. A week ago, he'd been avoiding her, refusing to get involved in her troubles. But what was going on between her and his father kept him from being neutral. She might have been foolish to marry his brother, but she didn't deserve to lose her son because Siggy had lost his.

"I can't."

"What's stopping you?" The question came out with a sardonic spin. "You have no ties to LA. In Vegas you have me."

She opened her mouth and looked ready to refuse.

He could almost see the wheels turning. Was she trading one bad situation for another? He could have reassured her, but no matter what else had happened between them, he'd always been honest with her.

"I don't like the idea of you and Dylan alone here." Trent couldn't imagine returning to Las Vegas and leaving her to fend for herself. "And I don't trust Siggy."

She gripped her keys tight and looked a little like a defendant awaiting a verdict. "How long will it take to sort out what's going on with the company?"

"I don't know. It will depend on what Logan finds in the company's files."

"I suppose I could find an inexpensive rental in Vegas."

"I think you and Dylan would be better off staying with me."

"Absolutely not."

"I live in a gated community, on an estate with two acres of land and a guesthouse. My housekeeper loves children and is completely trustworthy. Rhoda can watch Dylan whenever you need her to."

Although he thought he'd made a terrific pitch, Savannah looked unconvinced. "I don't understand."

"What's there to understand?"

"We haven't spoken since I married Rafe. Just yesterday I had to hunt you down in the club because you wouldn't answer any of my calls. Now you're bending over backward to help me out. I don't get it."

He didn't want to dig too deep into his motivations. "Don't look a gift horse in the mouth."

"You'll have to do better than that."

"What do you want me to tell you?"

She cocked her head and regarded him through narrowed eyes. "What changed? Why are you suddenly my knight in shining armor again?"

"I'm not." But he could see where she might be misinterpreting his helpfulness. "My motives are purely selfish."

"How, exactly?"

"Didn't you see the look on my father's face?" The memory of it made Trent grin. "He is beyond frustrated that I'm helping you."

"So this is about you and your father?"

"Yes." And in the spirit of honesty, Trent continued, "I also feel responsible for you getting involved with my brother and in this mess."

"Why do you think that?"

"You obviously were in a vulnerable place after we broke up, and Rafe took advantage of that."

She stared at him for a long moment before nodding. "I'd better go get Murphy and our things."

"Does that mean you're coming with me to Las Vegas?"

"It makes sense for the time being." She didn't appear happy or relieved.

"Why don't you stay here with Dylan and I'll take care of collecting your stuff?"

She shook her head. "Is it weird that I'm uncomfortable waiting in this parking lot alone?"

Trent realized then what a good job she'd been doing

hiding her anxiety. "Not weird at all. Grab Dylan and we'll do this together."

Ten minutes after she'd checked out and left the babysitter's suitcase with the concierge, they were headed back to the Van Nuys airport. Both she and Trent had been driving rental cars. They dropped them off at the agency before heading to the chartered plane.

All through the day, from the plane ride to their confrontation with Siggy and now a second flight, Dylan had proven to be a sunny, spirited child. Trent sat across from the boy and regarded him in bemusement. "He takes after you."

"He definitely has my nose."

"Yes, but that's not what I was referring to. I meant his temperament."

"What about his temperament?"

"Dylan is a happy baby. Rafe was a fussy child. At least that's what my mother says. And he turned into a difficult adult."

"Your brother had his moments." Savannah kept her attention fixed on Dylan. "I don't know how I got so lucky with Dylan. He's been easy since the day he was born." She laughed. "Makes me want to have several more."

Whenever she'd made statements like this, Trent visualized her surrounded by little girls with heart-wrenching blue eyes and blond ringlets. For some reason, he'd never pictured her with boys. Yet here sat a handsome lad with dark brown hair and curious blue eyes, and Trent wondered how many more sons were in her future.

"You're an excellent mother. Of course, that's no surprise to anyone."

"It was a surprise to me," she said. "As much as I've always wanted a family, I really wasn't sure if I was capable of taking care of one."

Her confession surprised him. "But you've always seemed so determined…"

How had she been so eager to do something when she wasn't sure if she could? Trent had always been confident in everything he did. He couldn't imagine taking on something he knew he couldn't handle. With her inability to stick up for herself, she'd always struck him as insecure and unwilling to take chances. Maybe she was braver than he'd ever realized.

"Just because I'm scared of something doesn't mean I won't do it. If that had been the case, I never would've gone to New York City. Never modeled. And I sure wouldn't have acted on a soap opera." She gave him a melancholy smile. "I didn't believe I could do any of it. Especially after I saw how beautiful the other girls were and heard the stories of how hard the modeling business was."

"When you left LA, I never imagined you doubted yourself. Why would you? You were beautiful."

"I was short."

"You're five-eight."

"Most models are five-ten and taller. I didn't book a lot of jobs because of that. And it kept me off the runway. Which made me feel inadequate. It's why I traded modeling for acting."

"How did I not know you felt this way?"

"I saw the girls you dated. Not only were they beautiful, but they were also over-the-top confident. They had to be to keep up with you."

But none of those girls had stuck. None of them lingered in his thoughts like Savannah had. Like she still did.

"What do you mean, keep up with me?"

"You know, your party lifestyle. The clubs, the celebrities you hang with. All that can be pretty intimidating for a girl with small-town roots, raised in the servants' quarters."

"I never saw you like that."

"I saw me like that." She tickled her son and made him giggle.

Trent let her words sink in. Why, in all the years they'd known each other, had she never spoken of this? She made it sound as if she didn't think she was good enough for him. That wasn't true. The trouble in their relationship had been that they wanted different things.

Besides, she'd considered herself good enough for his brother. Or was it that Rafe had never made her feel less than utterly desirable and truly wanted? A vise clamped down on Trent's chest.

"Well, you shouldn't."

He checked his watch and then turned his attention to the darkening sky outside the aircraft. They would be on the ground in twenty minutes. Trent could feel Savannah watching him, sensed her desire for him to elaborate, but he had no more to say.

An hour later, he was carrying his sleeping nephew through his house. Before taking her out to the guesthouse, Trent gave Savannah a tour of the wide-open first-floor living area.

Despite her years in his father's mansion and her year and a half living in her own enormous house, for some reason she was goggling at Trent's nine-thousand-square-foot spread.

"You live here?"

He wasn't sure what to make of the laughter in her voice. "Obviously."

"It's a little over-the-top, don't you think?"

"I bought it for the outdoor space," he explained, feeling slightly peevish at her criticism.

While the traditional French country style wasn't his cup of tea, the amenities more than made up for the elaborate plasterwork on the fireplaces and overabundance of pillars and crown molding. Floor-to-ceiling windows and French doors filled the house with light. The place had come furnished with faux antiques that complemented the builder's vision of a French château.

"I can't wait to see it."

Trent guided her through a set of French doors that let out onto a wide, covered terrace. In addition to the guesthouse, his backyard hosted a large pool with a swim-up bar and a pool house, an outdoor movie screen and a putting green. Savannah put on the brakes as soon as she stepped outside.

"Is that a slide?" She pointed out the towering water slide that spiraled from the second-floor terrace to the pool. "I'm not sure this is going to work out for Dylan and me."

"Why not?"

"It's a big boy playground." And from the way she was looking at him, he was the big boy.

"What does that have to do with anything?"

"Don't you think having your sister-in-law and her infant son living in your guesthouse will cramp your style?"

"I'm not planning on throwing any wild parties while you're here, if that's what you're insinuating."

She sighed and gave him her full attention. "We'll stay just a couple days. Long enough for me to get my feet back under me and to find a place we can rent for a little while."

"Stay as long as you want," Trent said and meant every word. "Now that that's settled, are you ready to see the guesthouse?"

Six

Shaded by the palm trees that dotted the landscape, Savannah sat beside Trent's pool with her feet dangling in the lukewarm water. No breeze stirred the air and sweat trickled down her skin. She was ready for the break in the heat the forecasters promised for later in the week. Apparently in the weeks leading up to Halloween, the highs in Las Vegas dropped from upper nineties to low eighties.

Beside her on the terra-cotta tile sat a plate with half a tuna sandwich and a glass of iced tea. Nearby, Dylan slept peacefully in a portable crib and Murphy snored happily on a shaded lounge chair. They'd been living in Trent's guesthouse for four days. With his backyard as gorgeously landscaped as any five-star resort, Savannah felt as if she was on vacation, not in the midst of a personal crisis.

She felt safe for the first time since she'd found out that Rafe was sick. Already her guards were coming down. Which troubled her because she hadn't only been motivated by fear of what Siggy might try next when she let Trent talk her into returning to Las Vegas. She'd also been swept up in a giddy euphoria that he'd cared enough to worry about her. In short, Savannah's reasons for coming to Las Vegas were more about what might happen with Trent than what had happened with Siggy.

Today she would stop procrastinating and corner Trent about what was going on with the label. She knew he and his friend had been digging into the company's files, and she needed to know what they'd found. But given the way he'd avoided answering her inquiries so far, she worried that what they'd found was really bad.

Just then, Trent came out onto the patio from the main house. Over the past few days, Savannah had noticed more and more that if she thought hard enough about Trent, he either appeared or called. In the old days she might have thought this meant they were in sync. These days she chalked it up to her infringement on his bachelor lifestyle.

"You look happy," he said, keeping his voice low as he approached. Today he wore a pair of khaki pants and a white polo that brought out his tan. His blue eyes flicked toward Dylan's crib. "I think Vegas agrees with you."

"I think what agrees with me is feeling safe for the

first time since Rafe died and I found out how bad our financial situation really was."

"It's going to be okay."

She studied his features and felt reassured by his sincerity. "Can you tell me what you found out about the business?"

"It's as you expected. The financials are not in good shape. They haven't been paying their artists everything they're owed. One or two probably won't sign another contract."

"What can we do?"

"West Coast Records has several strong artists. But there are too many who've done nothing. It's not their fault. They weren't well managed. A few of them could be kept on, provided their next albums are better produced."

"But who's going to do that? I don't know anything about the music side of things. I might be able to run the business side with help, but when it comes right down to it, the label needs someone like you who can do both."

"I know what you're thinking, but it's not going to happen. My father will never allow me to take over the company."

"Not even if you can save it from going under?"

"From the correspondence between him, Gerry and Rafe, Siggy doesn't believe the company is in trouble."

"How is that possible? Surely even if Rafe kept how bad it was from him, Gerry would have told Siggy the truth."

"And been the one to shatter the old man's vision of his perfect firstborn son?"

Savannah heard the bitterness in Trent's voice. No matter what he said to the contrary, it still stung that his father showed him so little respect.

"Besides," Trent continued, "Gerry has had his own agenda these past couple of years."

Not liking the sound of that, Savannah asked, "What sort of agenda?"

"Some of the company's troubles stem from Gerry's embezzling."

"Embezzling?" Savannah shook her head, unable to believe what she was hearing.

"Apparently he's been stealing money from the company for years. He's been in the perfect position to steal and hide it. I'm sure as years went on and he wasn't caught he grew bolder. And when he was passed over for CEO in favor of Rafe, he probably figured he'd get whatever he could and get out."

"What do we do? Do we call the police?"

"Unfortunately Gerry is a lot cleverer than my father ever gave him credit for. Not only did he steal money, he made it look as if Rafe took it. Only by digging into Gerry's finances was Logan able to find out that Gerry's spending outpaced his salary and bonuses."

Savannah's hopes plummeted. Nothing they'd found helped her situation. The company was likely on the verge of bankruptcy and so was she.

"Come on," Trent said, stripping off his shirt as he headed toward the pool house. "Let's go for a swim."

When she'd packed for Vegas the first time, she hadn't planned to be vacationing. "I don't have a suit."

The most she'd done in the last few days was to wade in the shallow end of the pool so that she could let Dylan frolic in the water. Given how hot the last few days had been, this hadn't been satisfying, but she'd been reluctant to venture off the property and go shopping for herself.

"I keep all sorts of suits in the pool house," Trent replied, disappearing into the building. Less than a minute later, he was back wearing swim trunks, his glorious chest and abs bare to the sun. "Try one of these."

It did not surprise Savannah one bit that the bikinis Trent held up were on the tiny side. "I don't suppose you have a one-piece in there somewhere."

He shook his head. "The last thing you need is a one-piece. You have a gorgeous body. You should show it off."

She'd had a gorgeous body. Now she carried a little extra weight on her hips and knew Trent liked his girls lean and fit. Almost as soon as the thought arrived, she dismissed it. What did it matter how Trent liked his women? She wasn't one of them. With a heartfelt sigh, Savannah got to her feet and took the bikinis Trent held out.

"I know he's sleeping, but could you keep an eye on Dylan while I change?"

After what had happened in LA, she was having a hard time letting Dylan out of her sight. If Trent had noticed her paranoia, he hadn't said anything. Savannah knew she would have to eventually leave her son in someone else's care, but for right now she was more comfortable keeping him close by.

Trent was peering at a sleeping Dylan when Savannah returned. In this unguarded moment Trent's expression captivated her. With his features softened in wonder, he looked younger and happier. Even though he didn't realize Dylan was his son, he was growing attached to the boy. This made Savannah's stomach tighten in an uncomfortable knot. Part of her wanted to tell Trent that he was Dylan's father. But would he believe her? Or would he see this as a ploy to manipulate him?

Better that the secret remain hidden. Trent liked his bachelor lifestyle and his freedom. No reason to disrupt either. She appreciated his help with the company and wouldn't burden him with the one thing he never wanted—a family.

"What?"

"Hmm?"

She came out of her thoughts and found him staring at her.

"You are looking at me funny. I'm not a complete idiot when it comes to kids, you know."

"You're not?" She retreated into friendly banter. "And where did you get all your experience?"

"For a couple months last year, I dated a woman who had two."

"Two what?"

"Two children. Agnes and Theo. They were four and eight. Great kids."

This news caused Savannah's confidence to implode. After everything he'd said about not wanting a family, he'd dated a woman with children. It felt like betrayal, which was ridiculous. He could date anyone he pleased. It was no business of hers. After all, she'd married his brother.

"That's nice." The urge to run over, pick up her son and hug him close was almost painful in its intensity. Savannah recognized her need for comfort.

"She was great. The kids were great."

"Sounds great."

"Aren't you going to ask me what happened?"

Savannah shook her head. "Are we going to swim or talk?"

Without waiting for his answer, she dived into the pool. The tepid water felt refreshing after the afternoon heat, and Savannah swam beneath the surface until her lungs burned. She rose, snatched a quick breath and dived again. Not until her fingers touched the pool's far wall did she come up again. Sucking in huge gulps of air, she turned and pushed off to stroke back the way she'd come.

Damn Trent for making her feel jealous. She had no right to the emotion where he was concerned. Most of the women she pictured him with were young party girls. She'd never imagined him dating someone with baggage. In the back of her mind a distressed voice called, *Why not me?*

At some point during her frantic swim, Trent had entered the pool. He stood near the center, his expression unreadable as she approached. Savannah stopped several feet away and gazed toward the portable crib. Through the mesh sides, she could see Dylan sleeping peacefully.

"She didn't mean anything to me."

Savannah couldn't believe Trent was continuing the conversation. "Really, it's none of my business."

"It was six months after you and I broke up. I wanted to see what dating a woman with kids was like." Obviously, Trent was not going to let it go.

"And what was it like?"

"Not bad. Different. We didn't really date. More like hung out. Right off the bat she told me she wasn't interested in someone like me."

"A party boy?"

"She wanted someone she could build a future with."

Savannah knew what that was like. "But she dated you anyway."

"She'd been divorced about a year and was looking to getting her feet wet in the dating pool." Trent ran his fingers through his hair, making it stand up in all directions. "I met her at the club. We went out once and both of us knew right away it wasn't going to work out."

"But you kept seeing her."

"There was no pressure."

Savannah had tried to keep things free and easy while they'd dated, but she hadn't always been successful. In her heart, she'd longed for a future with him. A life filled with children and happiness.

"Why are you telling me all this?"

"I don't know."

"That's not like you. You always have a reason for what you do."

"I usually have a reason for what I do. Except when it comes to you."

"Trent—"

Before she could finish whatever it was that she'd been about to say, his arms went around her and his lips found hers. Held tight against his strong body, Savannah gave herself to the powerful emotions surging through her. With her fingers buried in his hair, she hung on for dear life as he devoured her mouth. The water gave her buoyancy and she floated in a bubble of joy.

She wanted him. She wanted this.

The privacy offered by the lush landscaping around the pool eased Savannah's doubts as Trent released the clasp holding her bikini top in place. She gasped as his lips drifted down her neck and settled over the wildly beating pulse in her throat. She wrapped her legs around his hips, feeling his erection hard against her stomach. His right hand came between them and settled over her breast while his other hand cupped her butt, lifting her partially out of the water.

She reveled in the sweep of his tongue over her nipple. It tightened into an aching peak as he laved it once more before pulling the hard bud into his mouth and sucking. She closed her eyes and let the delicious sensations wash over her. After the first time they'd made love, the passion she and Trent shared left Savannah convinced that they belonged together. But no matter how overpowering and all-consuming the connection was between them, Trent wasn't about to settle down and give her the life she craved.

Over the heartbeat thundering in her ears, she heard the soft sounds Dylan made as he stirred to wakefulness. Her hands had worked their way down Trent's torso to the waistband of his swim shorts. Desire clouded her mind, but Savannah's maternal instincts were stronger. With a shudder she broke off their kiss and pushed against Trent's shoulders.

"Dylan," she gasped, shuddering as Trent's fingertips grazed the edge of her bathing suit bottoms, tantalizing inches from where she ached. "He's waking up. I need to get to him."

Without a hint of reluctance or disappointment, Trent set her free. As she swam to the pool's edge, she wasn't sure whether to feel relief or regret that he was being so understanding. With conflicting emotions churning in her gut, Savannah quickly toweled off and went to check on her son.

Dylan was rubbing his eyes, but when she spoke his name, he looked up at her with a wide grin. Savannah's heart melted. How lucky she was to have such a wonderful baby boy. Hearing Trent emerge from the pool, she glanced over her shoulder at him. If she couldn't have the love of her life, at least she had his son.

"I'd better get back to the guesthouse so I can change him."

"Savannah, about what just happened…"

"There's no need to say anything." Her heart contracted at his need to make excuses. "It's always been like this between us."

"And that's it?"

"What more is there? Nothing else about our situation has changed. We're the same people who broke up two years ago because I wanted a family and you didn't."

"I guess we are." His neutral expression told her nothing. "It's just always been easy to forget our differences when I'm kissing you."

He was certainly right about that. And the more time she spent around him, the more likely they would be to indulge in their passion for each other. But there was no future in that. She needed to start thinking about where she was going and what she was going to do.

"Do you have some time this afternoon to start coming up with a plan for straightening out the company?"

"I have a couple of meetings at the club that should take me into early evening. How about we do a late dinner here?"

"Seven?"

"Sounds about right."

Savannah wrapped herself in a dry towel and then picked up Dylan. She offered Trent a bright smile that hid her heavy heart. "I'll see you then."

As soon as Savannah disappeared in the direction of the guesthouse, Trent dived back into the pool. To burn off some of his sexual frustration, he swam hard for several laps before levering himself out and flopping onto a nearby lounge chair. For the last four days he'd been tormented by Savannah's proximity. Night was the worst. Knowing she slept mere steps from his big empty bed had summoned every memory of their time together. To keep himself from acting on his fantasies about her, he'd taken to spending long hours at the club and not returning home until the sky lightened toward dawn.

All of which had simply stoked his hunger, making him unable to keep his hands off her moments earlier. And now he'd agreed to a late dinner under the guise of talking business.

With a growl, Trent got to his feet and headed inside. She would expect him to have answers, and if he couldn't provide any she might get frustrated enough to head back to LA and take Siggy on by herself. He needed to sort through their options. Just as important, he needed to chat with one of his partners in the club, Nate Tucker.

Trent showered and dressed in gray slacks and a bright blue shirt. His impulses pointed him toward the back of the house, where he might run into Savannah again. Cursing his weakness, Trent headed for his garage.

The gated community where he lived was a twenty-minute drive from the Cobalt. Negotiating the heavy Las Vegas traffic gave him plenty of time to ponder what had led up to that fantastic kiss in the pool. What had possessed him to tell Savannah about Karen? He wasn't the type to dredge up past romances. And to belabor the fact that he'd dated a woman with children could only hurt Savannah.

Had he hoped to reiterate that he wasn't a guy who wanted to be tied down with kids? An observer of the conversation might have wondered if Trent was trying to give the impression that he'd at least experimented with being a family guy.

When Trent got to Cobalt, instead of heading to his office at the club, he headed for the hotel's executive offices. JT Stone, owner of the hotel, was a brilliant businessman and would have solid advice about how to deal with the failing record label. The two men had bonded over similar experiences growing up with difficult fathers and running family businesses. In JT's case, he'd fought to regain control of the company that had been in the family for years and won. But in the end, he'd sold the family's overleveraged hotel chain to his cousin in order to own Cobalt free and clear. That JT's father had ended up in prison for fraud had been icing on the cake.

Trent approached JT's executive assistant. "Is he around?"

Nina nodded. "He has a meeting in half an hour, but he's free until then."

"Thanks." Trent stepped into the doorway that led to JT's office and knocked on the frame. "Nina said you have a couple minutes."

"Sure, come on in." JT stood and came around his desk to shake Trent's hand. "What's up?"

"I have a little business dilemma I'd like to talk to you about."

JT's expression lit with interest. He'd dealt with more than his share of business dilemmas in the last two years. Gesturing toward the comfortable sitting area near the large windows that overlooked Cobalt's extensive grounds, JT grabbed a couple bottles of water and joined Trent.

"What's going on?"

"You know how things are with me and the family company."

"Sure."

"My sister-in-law came to me a few days ago wanting my help. When my brother died, he left his controlling interest in the business to his son. That puts Savannah in a position of overseeing the majority shares."

"Let me guess—she asked you to step in as CEO."

"Not exactly. Both of us know there's no way my father would go for that. But she needs my help sorting out the company's various problems."

"Such as?"

"For one thing, they're not paying their artists all the royalties owed to them."

"Because they don't have the money?"

"The company has been doing poorly for years, but things got worse once my brother got sick." Trent cracked the seal on the bottle of water and drank. "Then there's the problem of embezzlement. West Coast Records' general manager has been stealing for quite a few years."

JT arched an eyebrow. "And you know this how?"

Trent gave a little shrug. "I might have had Logan digging around in their computers."

JT and Logan were related through marriage. Their wives were two of the three Fontaine sisters, who ran resort and hotel properties on the Strip. Trent had often wondered what it was like for JT to be married to his competition. His wife, Violet, managed two of the three Fontaine properties.

"Did Logan find anything else troubling?"

"I haven't spoken with him in a couple days, but it's possible." Trent rubbed his eyes, noting a mild twinge in his temple as he considered what else might be going wrong. "In the meantime, Savannah is deep in debt thanks to her husband's reckless spending, and the only asset she has is her major stake in a failing company."

"She should try to dump the company now before the word gets out."

"Unfortunately the way the corporation was set up, she has to get approval from the board in order to sell. And since my father controls the board, he's making things difficult for her."

"Why?"

"He wants control of his grandson and Savannah out of the picture."

JT nodded his understanding. "She's not willing to let that happen."

"Siggy isn't going to let Dylan go without a fight. He already made an attempt to kidnap his grandson."

"You're kidding, right?"

"I wish I was." Trent went on to share the details of their visit to the company and how they'd come back to find Savannah's hotel room empty. "She and Dylan are staying with me at the house. The whole thing really spooked her. She hasn't left the property since she arrived."

"But he can't actually force her to give up her son."

"No," Trent agreed, his mind running through all the things Siggy could do. "But he knows how to play dirty, and I wouldn't put it past him to take her to court over some sort of manufactured evidence that makes her appear as if she's a bad mother."

"But she could fight him."

"She doesn't have the resources for a prolonged battle."

JT was assessing him through narrowed eyes. Trent could read his thoughts easily enough. The owner of Cobalt was wondering why Trent wasn't doing everything in his power to help his sister-in-law fight.

"I've offered financial help," he explained, preempting the man's question. "She's being stubborn about taking money from me. I don't think she'd be living in my guesthouse if Siggy hadn't spooked her by having the nanny bring him Dylan without Savannah's permission."

"You guys go back a ways, don't you?"

"We dated." As much as Trent liked JT, he wasn't about to open up about his complicated relationship with his brother's widow.

But that didn't stop JT from asking. "And yet she married your brother?"

"Yeah." Trent would've liked to leave it at that, but JT was staring at him and didn't appear as if he was going to take Trent's brief response as a hint to drop it. "She wanted family. Kids. You know."

"Seems pretty cold of her to take up with your brother after you two stopped seeing each other."

Trent would never describe Savannah as cold. "I

don't know that she chose my brother to spite me. She'd always liked Rafe. And she got pregnant."

None of this showed Savannah in a flattering light, which didn't strike Trent as being fair. And yet, wasn't this exactly what he'd been thinking about her for the last year and a half? What was with his sudden urge to defend her?

"She's been through a lot," he concluded.

"She's pretty lucky to have you." JT's demeanor went from curious to brisk and businesslike. "So it sounds like the problem you're facing is this. Her son owns a majority share of a company that's going under and she has no way of selling the shares and raising the money she needs to pay off her husband's debts."

"You summed it up perfectly."

"But if I know you," JT said with a smile, "you've plotted half a dozen ways to get her out of her predicament."

"Actually, I've only come up with three. And I wanted to run them by you to see which you think might work out the best."

"Fire away."

Seven

Courtney Day's unflappable smile concealed Savannah's disappointment as she carried a glass of wine across Trent's enormous living room to Scarlett Fontaine. All afternoon Savannah had been alternately nervous and giddy about the upcoming alone time with Trent. Instead of an intimate dinner between just the two of them, Trent had shown up a half hour late with Logan Wolfe and his wife in tow. To hide her disappointment, Savannah had donned her alter ego and was playing the perfect hostess, the way she'd done a hundred times as Rafe's wife.

"It's really nice to meet you," Savannah said, in awe of Scarlett's beauty. She'd seen her dozens of times on TV, but the real woman was so much more charismatic. "I'm a huge fan."

"Ditto." Scarlett gave a little laugh at Savannah's expression. "What? You don't think I know who you are? I'll have you know *Loving New York* has been a total obsession of mine for years. I thought you were great on it."

"Thanks. It was an interesting three years."

"Do you miss it?"

"Sometimes. I thought about getting back into acting, but I'm not sure LA or New York is where I want to be." Savannah recognized she might not have a choice.

"I totally understand where you're coming from. I'm lucky I've been able to coordinate my filming schedule so I only have to be in LA once a week. It's been a bit of a challenge balancing the management of Fontaine Richesse with my acting career. Fortunately I have an amazing husband who supports me one hundred percent." Scarlett shot a heated glance toward the two men standing out on the terrace.

"Fontaine Richesse? You mean the hotel on the Strip?" Savannah's admiration for the woman went up several degrees. "You manage that and have an acting career?"

Scarlett's husky laugh echoed around the two-story living space. "I have excellent people in place to help me with the hotel, and my sister Violet is always on call if something comes up when I'm not around."

"Still." Savannah was feeling woefully inadequate. What had she done in the last year and a half? "I'm feeling overwhelmed and I'm not even working at the moment."

"But you have a baby to take care of, and you just

lost your husband. Plus from what Logan tells me, the company your son inherited is having all sorts of problems."

Savannah wasn't surprised Scarlett knew some of her background. After all, Logan was helping Trent. Obviously the couple would have talked on their way here, and Logan would've explained what the meeting was about.

"It's a bit of a mess," Savannah agreed. "I don't know what I'd do if Trent hadn't agreed to help me."

"How long have you two known each other?"

"My aunt is his father's housekeeper. I moved in with her when I was eleven."

"So you grew up with him?"

"Sort of. It's weird living in someone else's house and being separated by the whole employer/employee thing. I probably shouldn't have gotten to know Trent and his siblings as well as I did."

"Had you always been in love with his brother?"

"No." It was an awkward situation to try to explain. "Actually, Trent and I dated for a few years while I was living in New York." Perhaps *dated* was not quite the right term for what they had done. She knew he'd seen other women when they were apart. But every time they got together, he'd made her feel like she was his only one.

Scarlett's eyes widened a little at Savannah's confession. "That explains a lot. You sure know how to make things complicated."

"I don't try to complicate things," Savannah said,

"but they often seem to end up that way. I'm not very good at getting what I want."

"Maybe you just don't believe that you deserve to get it."

"You might be right." She'd never really believed that Trent would give up his bachelor ways for her. And that had kept her from fully committing to their relationship, as well. "I've always shied away from disappointment. It's kept me from going after what's really important."

"It's not too late."

"No, I suppose it's not." But she was lying.

Savannah glanced in Trent's direction once again. She'd really blown it with him when she'd agreed to marry his brother. If she'd chosen any other man, Trent might have been willing to give their relationship another chance. But Trent's resentment of his brother ran deep and her desperate decision had built an insurmountable wall between them. There was no going back from that.

Trent might be willing to help her, but that was because he had his own agenda when it came to West Coast Records. The chemistry between them might be as hot as ever, but in her heart she knew what had happened in his office last week and had almost happened today was more about looking backward than moving forward.

"I was planning on moving to Tennessee once I found someone to run West Coast Records," Savannah said. "But lately I'm not sure I belong there or that I belong anywhere." Her gaze drifted toward Trent.

"You should give Las Vegas a try. If you're still interested in acting, it's a short plane ride to LA."

"When I left New York, I intended to continue acting, but then Rafe and I got involved and he didn't want his wife to work."

"Do you have an agent?"

Savannah shook her head. "I had one in New York, but we parted ways when I moved to LA. I wasn't sure if I wanted to work in film or TV and figured I would do something about representation once I got to there. Only...things happened and I never did."

"I'll put you in touch with a couple agents I know. Either one would be great to represent you."

"Thank you."

To her surprise, she felt a flutter of excitement in her chest. She'd connected working as an actress with living in LA. Savannah had opened her eyes to other possibilities. If she worked in film, she might go on location anywhere in the world. Lots of actresses balanced children and careers. No reason why she couldn't.

"I'll bet Trent would like it if you stuck around Las Vegas."

"Once we get things sorted out with the company, I'm not sure he'll notice if I stick around or not." But was she being honest with herself or was this another attempt to protect herself from getting hurt again?

"You don't believe that." Scarlett regarded her somberly. "When my sisters got involved with JT and Ashton, I knew before anyone else that they belonged together. I get the same vibe when I look at you and Trent."

Savannah shook her head. "You've seen us together for less than a minute. How could you possibly tell anything about our relationship?"

"I've known Trent for two years, and Logan and I have been to his club a lot. I've never seen him look at any woman the way he looks at you."

Afraid of how much she wanted to believe Scarlett, Savannah gave a little laugh but decided not to argue. It didn't really matter how Trent looked at her. Two years ago, he hadn't wanted a future with her. In the meantime, she'd married his brother and given birth to Dylan. Trent might desire her—and that's probably what Scarlett was picking up on—but he most certainly was not going to give up his lifestyle and ask her to marry him.

And since that's what she wanted, wasn't she a fool to let herself get caught up in him once more? She needed to move out. That meant she had to stop burying her head in the sand, get a job and a place for her and Dylan to live.

"I'm really glad I met you," Savannah said. "I need to get back to work, and I'm thinking the sooner the better."

"I'm heading to LA in a couple of days. If you'd like to come along, I'd be happy to introduce you to some friends who could get you started on the right path."

Maybe by the time she got herself reestablished in LA the situation with Siggy would be less stressful.

And if not, a new source of income meant she could afford to fight him and keep her son safe.

Savannah smiled at Scarlett in appreciation. "That would be terrific."

Trent glanced over his shoulder and saw the two women engrossed in their conversation. "You were right," he told Logan, delighting at the rare smile curving Savannah's beautiful lips. "Savannah looks a lot more relaxed."

"My wife is like that. She has a knack for making people feel better. And if Savannah wants to go back to acting, Scarlett can help her out. She has some great contacts in Hollywood."

That made Trent frown. He hadn't considered that Savannah might return to LA so soon. It had only been a week since Siggy had pulled his stunt, and there was no reason to think he wouldn't try something equally despicable if Savannah and Dylan returned to LA.

His concern grew over dinner as Scarlett and Savannah chatted about the industry. It was apparent that his sister-in-law intended to return to work.

The two couples lingered over the meal and then moved outside for dessert. Trent hadn't done a lot of this sort of entertaining. A low-key evening with another couple was a nice change from the sort of parties he usually threw here. Between the game room in the upstairs loft that overlooked the living room and the big backyard with the pool, slide and outdoor movie screen, he usually hosted groups that liked to dance, drink and get a little crazy.

Savannah had taken a couple minutes as everyone moved outside to go check on her son. She came back with the baby monitor and explained she'd sent Rhoda home. The conversation between the women changed then to talk of babies and future plans for children.

Scarlett patted her husband's knee and shot him a sly smile. "We've decided to put off having children for at least another year. He's not happy about it, but I don't think my husband has any idea how demanding I'm going to get when I'm pregnant."

"It can't possibly be any worse than you are right now." Logan's words didn't match the tenderness in his eyes as he gazed at his gorgeous wife.

"Then you're in for a rude awakening. Violet was the sweetest thing until she got pregnant with Rowan. Poor JT was beside himself." Scarlett rolled her eyes in dramatic fashion.

"Beside himself with joy, maybe." Trent recalled JT being nothing but thrilled in the months leading up to becoming a father. He laughed at the sharp look Scarlett shot at him. "And Logan will be no different."

"You're not helping," Scarlett said, turning to Savannah. "I suppose you're going to side with them, too."

"I used to want a big family," Savannah said, not letting her gaze stray anywhere near Trent. "But now that I have Dylan, I'm content."

Trent felt an awkward *whump* in his chest. If he hadn't known better, he would've thought it was his heart breaking. Savannah was trying hard to spin her situation into something positive, but Trent had known her a long time and didn't believe for one minute that she would give up on her dreams unless they'd been crushed by disappointment.

"Melody and I are your family, too," he reminded her.

"I haven't forgotten. Which is why I've decided not to move to Tennessee."

"That's great."

"I'm glad you're okay with it," Savannah said, giving him a weak smile. "And if I can swing a few acting jobs in LA, I can afford a little house for Dylan and me here."

She made it sound as if she was intended to move out as soon as possible. "No need to rush. You can stay here as long as you want."

"I appreciate your generosity, but I think I've relied on you far too much already."

How did he explain to her that he liked it when she relied on him? When he came to her rescue she always gazed at him as if he was larger than life. In her eyes he was a hero, not the troublemaker everyone had to watch out for.

Trent kept an eye on the clock as the evening wound down. He'd hoped for some alone time with Savannah before she turned in, but the hour grew later and later. At long last, Scarlett patted her husband on the knee.

"I think you mentioned needing to get some more work done this evening," Scarlett said, standing up. "A security expert's job is never done."

"I think everyone here can sympathize," Trent said, trying to keep his relief from showing as everyone made their way to the foyer. "All of us have been known to work some pretty unorthodox hours."

"Thanks for the invite," Logan said. "Next time, let's do it at our house."

The two men shook hands while the women hugged. Minutes later, Trent and Savannah stood alone in his empty house. He wasted no time pulling her into his arms and kissing her. From her passionate response, she'd been feeling the same sensual pull. Her fingers tugged his shirt free from his pants and dived beneath the hem.

He groaned at the pleasure of her palms skating along his bare back. Lifting her into his arms, he made for the guesthouse, instinctively knowing she would want to be nearby if Dylan needed her. His frantic heartbeat made it hard for him to take things slow, but as he lowered her feet to the floor beside her bed, he sucked in a calming breath, pushed her out to arm's length and closed his eyes.

"Tonight we're going to take our time," he said, opening his eyes and peering at her.

She was flushed, her expression slightly dazed. She backed away and put her hands to her cheeks for a moment. Trent thought for sure she'd come to her senses. To his relief, instead of ordering him to leave her room, she stripped her asymmetrical tank over her head and cast it aside. Standing before him in a nude bra and khaki leggings, she threw her hands wide as if in surrender.

"I don't know if I can."

Trent loosened the buttons on his shirt and sent it sailing to join her top on the floor. "We have the rest of the evening to get it right."

Her pale eyebrows rose. "That's a relief, because I'm pretty sure we're seriously out of practice." She stuck her thumb inside the elastic waistband of her leggings and stretched them away from her body. "Would you like me to take these off, or do you want to do the honors?"

Trent's mouth went dry. He stepped into her space and bracketed her waist just above the material. Her smooth skin was warm beneath his palms. Moving with slow deliberation, he dipped his fingertips below her waistband. His hands rode her curves downward, taking her leggings with them. She was trembling as he helped her step out of the snug pants.

While she unhooked her bra and slipped it free, he dropped a kiss on her stomach. Eager to revisit every inch of her, he trailed his fingertips from her instep to her knee. Her breath grew shallow, uneven. She set her hands on his shoulders and leaned on him for support as her legs shook. Still kneeling, he hooked his fingers into her cream lace panties and eased them down her thighs.

"I don't know how much more of this I can take," she gasped as his mouth grazed down from her belly button.

"Let's see about that, shall we?"

Getting to his feet, Trent eased her back onto the bed and quickly divested himself of his clothes. She lifted onto her elbows to watch him, and he was aware of every greedy flicker in her blue gaze.

She propped one foot on the bed and waggled her knee in an enticing manner. "Come get me."

He hesitated only long enough to fish several condoms out of his pants pocket. She raised her eyebrow as he dropped them onto the nightstand.

"It's been too long," he said, setting his knee on the bed.

Her hands slid up his ribs and across his back as he covered her with his body. "Too long since what?"

"Since I've had you all to myself."

He kissed her then, stopping any further conversation and distracting her from the anguish behind what he'd said. She was all supple limbs and hot, welcoming mouth. Her tongue danced with his as they rediscovered each other with lips, teeth and hands. Nibbling his way down her neck, he found the sensitive spot made her writhe. Last time in his office, he'd been denied her beautiful breasts. He intended to make up for that.

A breathy moan broke from her lips as he swirled his tongue around her breast, making her back arch. She dug her fingers into his shoulders. Knowing exactly what she liked, he moistened her hard nipple and released a puff of air across the sensitive nub. Once again he was rewarded as her hips lifted. Her every moan, gasp and cry caressed his senses, the familiarity erasing their almost two-year estrangement.

Where once she'd been flawless, her body had now gained character. Motherhood had brought changes that he found vastly intriguing. He appreciated how her stretch marks testified to her maturity. And the extra weight she carried on her hips and butt lent her figure a lushness that enhanced her sensuality.

She protested when his fingers trailed across a

stretch mark on her belly. "Motherhood isn't kind to a woman's body."

He resisted when she tried bringing his hand back to her breast. "You are more beautiful than ever."

"Next you'll be telling me it's okay that I packed on the pounds."

"You've hardly done that. And I love every inch of you. I always have."

He slid his shoulders between her thighs and filled his palms with her round backside. Her whole body trembled as he grazed his lips along the hollow beside her hipbone, and a ragged laugh escaped her.

It had been too long. Far too long. He licked her then. Her hips bucked in reaction, so he put his palm flat on her belly to keep her still. Her trembling increased as he tasted her excitement and found her ready for him. He flicked his tongue the way she liked and she moaned. At the sound he smiled. Then, he hummed against her, knowing it made her crazy.

"Yes!"

He needed her to remember how it was between them. To be the only man she thought of. Pulling out every trick in the book, he made love to her with his mouth, hands and voice.

"I want to hear that noise again," he said, looking up to watch her expression.

"What noise?" She was almost too breathless to be understood.

"The one you make when I do this." He repeated his action and wrenched a soft yelp from her throat. "Yes," he purred, "just like that."

In the past, he'd utilized his expertise to bring her to the edge of orgasm and keep her there. Once, he'd even drawn this out for an hour. But tonight she came the instant he slid one finger inside her. With her lips parted on a strangled cry, her body bowed. The length and intensity of her climax caught him by surprise.

"Words cannot describe how amazing you are at that." A single tear slipped down the side of her face, and she brushed it away with the back of her hand before extending her arms to him. "Come up here and kiss me."

He obliged, but kept the contact light and sweet despite the temptation of her parted lips and the fingers she'd tunneled through his hair.

"I'm going to return the favor, I promise," she said, grasping his bicep with surprising force. "As soon as I've recovered."

"Later."

Trent reached to the nightstand and after two futile attempts managed to grab a condom with his shaking fingers. He caught the wrapper between his teeth and carefully tore it open. Hollowed out by the longing to be inside her, he sheathed himself in the protection and suckled her breasts as he settled between her thighs.

If the tantalizing movement of her hands down his body was intended to drive him mad, it worked. And based on the look she cast from beneath her lashes, she knew just how well. He didn't care. His level of arousal was almost painful as she wrapped her long fingers around him. A groan tore from his throat.

Fighting the urge to drive into her heat, he unclenched his teeth long enough to gasp, "I promised we'd take our time." He pulled her hand away from his erection. "I'm too close for much of that."

"Not close enough." Her pout made him smile.

Their lips came together again. The kisses were slow and sweet, a blending of tongue and breath. The mood shifted from frantic hunger to wrenching emotion. It was easy to forget the distance and hurt that had separated them.

Savannah slid the sole of her foot over Trent's muscled calf and let her hands roam over his chiseled torso. Each rise and dip of his glorious body was imprinted on her memory, but the real thing was so much better.

With her body building slowly toward another mindblowing orgasm, Savannah stormed Trent's mouth with her tongue and nipped at his lower lip. She rocked against him until he flexed his fingers on her hip and shuddered. His erection lay trapped against her belly, hot and eager for her. Her hands dived between them and stroked him.

"I can't wait another second. I need you inside me."

"I need that, too." His voice rasped against her neck. "It's been too long."

When he shifted over her, she spread her legs and lifted her hips. Her head fell back and her breath caught as he positioned himself and thrust.

Stars exploded behind her eyes. "Magic," she murmured, closing her eyes to glory in how her body stretched and adapted to accommodate him. The fit was always perfect. He was her match in this.

"How I've missed this." Trent seized her mouth and began to move.

It wasn't like the night in his office when they'd both been hungry and frantic. This time Trent stared into her eyes and laced his fingers with hers. The emotion shading his expression was so raw it threatened to rip her heart out. Savannah wanted to turn aside and not get sucked into the whirlpool of longing for things that could never be.

Trent would never want more than this. She'd learned to accept that, but at moments like these when he gave her everything he was, her foolish heart hoped that maybe this time it would be different. Shutting the door on such thoughts, she closed her eyes and let her other senses take over.

His ragged breath fanned her hot skin as he kissed her shoulder. They were both close. She recognized the tension in his muscles and the rising intensity of his low murmurings. He wanted her to come and wouldn't let himself go until she did. Her climax waited, just out of sight. She was holding back, unwilling to reach for her pleasure, wanting to prolong the intimacy of the moment just a little while longer.

But her body wasn't about to be controlled. The first sharp bite of her orgasm stopped her breath. Her eyes snapped open. She caught Trent's satisfied smile as he watched her. The sight of him was enough to send her over the edge. Pleasure reared up and slapped her hard. Savannah exploded.

Trent's muted exclamation came a second later. Savannah had a moment to appreciate that he'd kept his voice down in consideration of Dylan sleeping in the room next door before a second wave of pleasure rolled through her.

She was sunk. The pressure in her chest told her that what had happened tonight had opened a rift in her defenses she'd be helpless to patch. It would take time and space to heal, and she wasn't sure she had the willpower to let either do its work.

In the aftermath of their lovemaking, Trent rolled over so that she was lying on top of him. He sent his fingertips skating along her spine in long, soothing caresses. She loved this part. The moments when Trent's guard was still down and she could talk to him about anything. But tonight she had trouble thinking of a subject that wouldn't lead to trouble.

Trent was the first to speak. "I'm sorry I was so angry with you for marrying Rafe."

"We'd been broken up for months. And it had ended so badly. But I shouldn't have started seeing Rafe."

"I couldn't believe how fast you got over me."

She was surprised by his admission. "I didn't get over you." She frowned. "You were the one who didn't want me."

"That's not true."

Trent shifted them until they lay on their sides facing each other, legs tangled to maintain their connection. Savannah put her head on the pillow while he caressed her cheek. Her heart thumped erratically as she took in his somber expression.

"You told me you had no interest in getting married and having children," she reminded him.

"That didn't mean I didn't want you. I just didn't

want the same things you did." He kissed her forehead. "You were the one who decided to end our relationship. Not me."

Savannah remembered how she'd ached the day she'd told him they were done. "I guess in the end, it doesn't matter which of us called it quits. The fact is, we wanted different things and neither of us would be happy long term."

"I don't believe that's true. I would've been happy with you." The simple words sounded as if they came straight from his heart.

"But you didn't want…" *Children. Marriage.*

"I felt backed into a corner by your expectations."

"By my…?" She was horrified. If she could have put her dreams aside and been satisfied to just love Trent, would they have stayed together? She grew lightheaded at the thought of all the heartache she could've avoided. "How is that possible? I never put pressure on you."

"No, you didn't. At least not intentionally. But you had such an idealistic view of how you wanted your life to be." His fingers toyed with a strand of her hair, tickling her shoulder. "Were you happy with my brother?"

"Our marriage was more about an understanding than passion." She read no tension or hostility in his body as his hands played over her skin with lazy contentment. "He didn't love me."

"Did you love him?"

"Not the way a wife should. As I said, we both went in with our cards on the table. He wanted Dylan to carry on your father's dynasty." She shifted her head and kissed Trent's bare shoulder.

"And you were okay with that?"

"I was scared and alone and pregnant. I didn't know what I was going to do." Remembering that time, Savannah winced. That woman had been forlorn and in desperate need of saving. "I auditioned for anything that came along, but no one wanted to hire a woman who was three months pregnant. And I was sick. All the time. They talk about morning sickness. I had all-day sickness."

"I'm sorry it was such a hard time for you. And I'm glad my brother was there to help."

Rescuing her had always been Trent's thing. She could hear the regret in his voice and lifted her head to gaze into his eyes.

"He would have loved to hear you say that."

Trent scowled and gave her hair a fond tug. "You always see the best in people." He sounded like a weary big brother. "That's what gets you into trouble."

"I know you and Rafe never got along because of how your father favored him, but he wasn't a villain." Savannah wasn't sure why she needed Trent to recognize an alternate view of his brother. "He was as hurt and frustrated as you were. Siggy dumped the entire burden of his expectations and the weight of West Coast Records' legacy on Rafe. I'm not sure you realize how lucky you were to escape."

From his closed expression, she could tell he didn't believe her.

"Rafe wanted the business and he got it."

One thing marrying Rafe had done was give her a front-row seat to the dysfunction of the Caldwell household. During the short months she'd been Rafe's wife, she'd learned how much he'd been bothered by the rivalry Siggy had created.

"You're right, but he didn't want to be in it alone. He recognized that he needed your ability to scout new talent and Melody's talents as a songwriter and producer. Siggy ruined his dream as much as he destroyed yours."

"If you're trying to convince me to like my brother, you're wasting your time."

"It's not about you liking Rafe." Savannah laid her cheek against his chest once more. "It's about how the bitterness you carry for him keeps you stuck in the past."

If Trent understood that Rafe had been Siggy's tool, he might one day release some of the resentment that made him keep people at a distance. Maybe he'd stop running from love.

From her.

From being a family with her and Dylan.

Hopelessness swept over her. But could Trent ever see her son as anything other than his brother's child? And what would happen if he learned the truth? Would he hate her or could he understand why she'd chosen not to tell him?

Savannah kissed Trent, letting her love for him ignite her passion once more. His ardent response pushed her anxiety to the far reaches of her mind. She had time to sort everything out. Now all she wanted to concentrate on was this moment and this man.

Eight

"It's so good to see you," Savannah said, hugging her sister-in-law.

Because of Melody's touring schedule, Savannah hadn't seen her since Rafe's funeral. For the past year she'd been traveling around the country opening for Nate Tucker and his band. Melody had lost weight but gained a little rock 'n' roll flair. Dressed all in black, she wore a flared leather skirt and lacy T-shirt with ankle boots. Formerly happy to write songs and stay in the background, she'd resisted when Nate set out to convince her to open for his band. But the singer/song-writer/producer was nothing if not persistent when he recognized talent—in addition to being part owner of Club T's, Nate had started his own record label and had a recording studio downtown.

"I'm excited to be in Las Vegas and can't wait to get into the studio to put the finishing touches on my first album."

"When do I get to hear some of it?"

"Soon," Melody promised, her gaze darting to one side. "I wrote a couple more songs that I want to get into the studio and record. After that I'll go through what I have and see what might work for the album."

"I'm sure they're going to be fantastic. All of them."

"Where's my nephew?" Melody asked. "I thought after what my father did you'd have a hard time letting him out of your sight."

"Trent has him in the pool." Savannah kept her expression as neutral as possible beneath Melody's wide-eyed regard. "He's teaching him how to swim, if you can believe it."

"I can't believe you're here," Melody said. "At Rafe's funeral, you and Trent were on opposite sides of the room from each other the entire day. What changed?"

"Your brother and I have sort of come to an understanding. I can thank your father for that. I wouldn't be here if there wasn't trouble with West Coast Records. And if Siggy hadn't threatened me with taking Dylan away."

"It seems like there's more going on here than just a simple understanding." Melody put special emphasis on the last word and gave Savannah a knowing look. "I mean, you're living with him."

"In the guesthouse," Savannah explained. "And you're right—there's more going on. Rafe's and my finances were really bad. I'm almost a million dollars in debt. And until I'm working again, I have no income to live on."

"What are you going to do?"

"My plan is to go to LA tomorrow with Scarlett Fontaine. Thanks to her, I've set up three interviews with agents."

"Who's watching Dylan while you're interviewing?"

"I'm leaving him with Trent's housekeeper. She's been terrific."

"Oh, good. Since you're leaving him here, then I can pitch in. I need a little practice taking care of a baby."

Savannah stared at Melody in confused silence, unsure if she should voice the first thing that popped into her mind. "I'd love for you to spend some time with Dylan. But why do you need practice?"

"I'm pregnant." Melody offered up a tremulous smile. "Yikes."

"That's great. I'm so happy for you and Kyle."

"Well, you can be happy for me."

From the tenor of Melody's response, Savannah sensed not all was well. "Kyle isn't happy? How is that possible? He adores you."

"I haven't told him yet."

Savannah closed her eyes briefly, recalling the confusing muddle of uncertainty and joy when she realized she was pregnant.

"You know he's going to be great about this."

"I don't know that. We haven't been together that long and haven't talked about marriage. I don't know where he stands on the whole kid thing."

"How far along are you?"

"Barely six weeks. I took a long weekend off from the tour and flew to LA for his birthday. It was a fantastic three days." Her eyes glowed with heartbreaking fondness for several seconds before dimming. "And then Nate called to say that they'd added an extra two weeks to the tour and Kyle got so mad. He complained about how much time we'd been apart and told me to quit. We had a huge fight." She trailed off, looking miserable.

"But he was all for it. He's been one hundred percent behind your career from the very beginning."

Melody gave a little shrug. "I don't think either one of us realized how hard it was going to be to be apart." She sat down and put her hands in her lap. "He's been so distant these last few months. I don't know what's gotten into him. I'm worried he doesn't love me anymore."

"That's impossible. I've seen you two together. He adores you."

Melody pressed her lips together, shifted on the couch and heaved a huge sigh. "A month ago, he practically accused me of cheating on him with Hunter Graves."

Savannah understood why Kyle might be worried. "Because of that photo of the two of you holding hands as you left that New York club?" She'd wondered what was up after seeing the image, even though she knew without a doubt that Melody would never risk her relationship with Kyle. "Okay, I'm sorry, but I could see where he might have gotten the impression that you and Hunter were together."

"But we're just friends. Nothing more. It was a madhouse as we left. Hunter grabbed my hand so we wouldn't be separated on the way to the car."

"You dated him on and off for a year and a half before you and Kyle got together."

In fact, at one point Melody had tried to use Kyle to make Hunter jealous. The plan had backfired, but in the best way possible. The ruse had awakened Kyle's true feelings for Melody and made her realize the man she was meant to be with had been right under her nose.

"And I was miserable," Melody said. "Why would Kyle think I would go back to that?"

"Maybe you should talk to Kyle about all this. Tell him how you feel."

Given her own situation, Savannah wasn't the best person to be offering relationship advice, but she felt compelled to say something that might ease her friend's mind.

"I don't know, but we haven't spoken more than a half-dozen times in the last three months."

And Savannah knew that wasn't like them. "You need to talk to him about this."

"I will. I promise. But I really need to get the album finished first."

"How long do you think that's going to take?"

Melody had been living with Kyle three months before going on tour with Nate. They'd been dating for six months before she moved in with him. And before that, they'd known each other and been friends since high school. Kyle had been Trent's best friend since they'd met freshman year, and Savannah had known

Kyle from all the times he'd hung out with Trent. She hadn't been surprised when Melody and Kyle finally got together.

Melody looked uncomfortable. "I don't know."

"The longer you wait, the worse it's going to be." Since Rafe's death, at least once a day Savannah regretted not telling Trent the truth about Dylan when she first learned she was pregnant. She'd kept quiet because she'd been afraid to get hurt again. Which had been silly, because she'd lost Trent anyway.

"You're right. But if I go to LA and tell him, I'll know how he reacts. If I stay here and finish the album, I can pretend for a while that when he finds out he's going to be thrilled."

Melody was operating with the same faulty logic Savannah had used. It had backfired for her; she could only hope that the same didn't happen to her good friend.

"He is going to be thrilled," Savannah assured her, trusting that truth. "He loves you."

"Sometimes love isn't enough." Melody stared at her hands.

Savannah's voice rang with conviction. "And sometimes it's all you need."

Their conversation was interrupted by the appearance of Trent and Dylan, with Murphy trotting along beside them. As always when Savannah saw father and son together, her heart gave a big bump.

"How'd his swimming lesson go?" she asked, holding her arms out for Dylan's towel-wrapped body.

Trent showed no inclination to give up Dylan. "He's

already learned how to hold his breath when he goes underwater." He leaned forward to kiss Melody on the cheek. "It's good to see you."

"It's good to see you, too." She looked a little startled by her brother's sunny demeanor and shot a sidelong glance in Savannah's direction. "I hope it's okay if I crash here for a couple weeks while I finish my album. Unless it's too crowded?"

"I have plenty of room. When is Kyle coming? I'll make a couple tee times to get him out of your hair."

"He's not going to come this trip." Melody made a stab at looking undisturbed, but couldn't quite pull it off.

Her brother frowned. "Why not?"

Savannah decided it might be easier for Melody to have this conversation with her brother if they were alone. "I'm going to change Dylan."

With Trent focused on his sister, Savannah had an easy time making her escape. She dressed her son in dry clothes and wondered what Trent would make of his sister's situation. He had demonstrated the same sort of protectiveness with Savannah as he had with Melody. Especially when it came to her relationship with his best friend.

While he and Kyle had always been the best of friends, Trent hadn't been wild about Melody dating him. But since she was a strong-minded woman in her twenties, with a successful career and clear idea of whom she was getting involved with, Trent's warnings had been unwelcome.

To distract herself from what was going on in the

main house, Savannah took stock of her limited wardrobe and began planning for the upcoming interviews in LA. She was still operating with the same suitcase of clothes she'd brought to Las Vegas the first time. While preparing to sell the house, she'd packed up the bulk of her wardrobe and put it in storage with the idea that she would sort through it as soon as she'd gotten settled.

Dylan's swim had taken the edge off his energy, and he was content to sit on the floor in her closet and play with his musical bear. By pushing on the bear's right paw, he was able to scroll through the playlist until he found his favorite song. Then he waved his hands and sang along in his cute baby way while Murphy barked and growled at the noisy toy.

"Why am I not surprised that he's musical." Trent's voice came from the doorway. "I hope you don't mind that I let myself in."

"I don't mind. This is your house. And that's why I've been thinking that maybe Dylan and I should move out."

"Move out? Why?"

"Melody needs the peace and quiet of the guest-house in order to finish her album."

"Where are you thinking about going?"

"I thought something nearby." She paused. "Or LA."

Trent's eyebrows crashed together. "Have you forgotten the reason you moved in here in the first place?"

"I haven't forgotten."

Trent thought she'd come to Las Vegas to keep Dylan safe, but that wasn't the only reason. She'd foolishly hoped that once Trent spent time with her and

Dylan that he'd miraculously decide that being a family with them was all he wanted.

"But things are different now," she continued. "And depending on how my auditions go in the next couple days, I might need to be closer to make the most of the opportunities."

"That's not the tune you were singing two days ago, and don't give me the excuse about Melody. You knew she was coming. Why the sudden change of heart?"

Savannah couldn't explain the real reason to him: the awkwardness of living in his guesthouse and wanting to be more than just a convenient fling. Falling in love with him all over again wasn't good for either of them. For a second, Savannah's chest became tight and her lungs refused to work. She searched for calm.

It was good for Dylan that she and Trent were getting along, but keeping things friendly and uncomplicated would be best. In addition, she needed to stop relying on Trent to save her and stand on her own two feet.

"I guess it comes down to not having a plan and not having much in the way of options because of my financial situation. What Siggy did spooked me. I reacted before thinking everything through."

"There's no reason to believe he won't try something again."

"That's why I'm leaving Dylan here while I meet with agents. I know he'll be safe with you."

"I don't understand why you're so determined to get back to work. You're more than welcome to stay here as long as you want."

"That's generous of you, but I really need to move forward with my life." And if it wasn't going to be with Trent, then she needed to put some distance between them as soon as possible. "And speaking of Melody, have you spoken with her about what's going on between her and Kyle?"

"She said they're having a little trouble." He ran his hand through his hair and his mouth tensed. "She warned me to leave things alone and mind my business."

"She's right. Melody's a big girl. She doesn't need her brother messing in her love life."

"So what am I supposed to do? Sit by and let her be miserable?"

"Why don't you focus on what we're going to do about West Coast Records and let Melody sort out her own problems? If she wants you to step in, she'll say so."

"Fine. I found a guy who can take over running the company. I'll text you his number so you can meet with him while you're in LA. I think you'll like him."

"That's wonderful. I'll look forward to talking with him. And if I want to hire him, do you have a plan for how to get him past Siggy and Gerry?"

"If things go the way I think they will, you won't have to."

Savannah shook her head. "Will it do me any good to ask you what you have planned?"

"Grab dinner with him at Cuts Beverly Hills."

"So your father will get wind of the meeting?"

"Exactly. The restaurant's practically in his backyard, and he's sure to hear if you show up."

"And then what? We sit around and wait?"

"If I know my father, we won't have to wait for long."

Pushing a stroller that contained his sleepy nephew, Trent sauntered into the recording studio of Nate Tucker's indie label, Ugly Trout Records. Since Savannah had left for LA this morning, Trent had been feeling edgy and out of sorts. While he knew it was important to her that she get back to work, he couldn't help but feel as if it was a huge mistake for her to think about returning to LA. After what had happened the week before, he'd assumed she would hide out in Las Vegas with him at least until they figured out how to handle Siggy. Trent's intention was to untangle Savannah from his father's company. Today, he was going to present to Nate an idea for how to go about that.

The receptionist directed Trent to studio B, where Melody and Nate were doing some recording for her album. When Trent entered the studio's production booth, Nate's gaze flicked over his two visitors before returning to Melody.

Trent leaned against the wall and listened to his sister. Accompanied by a guy in a knit cap playing the guitar, she sat at an electric piano, her strong, pure voice pouring out a song of heartbreaking angst. The uncomplicated arrangement allowed her songwriting to shine. Trent felt the hairs rise on the back of his neck at the emotion resonating through the lyrics. What was going on with his baby sister?

As she finished the song, Nate blew out a breath and

rocked back in his chair. "She sounds amazing. This album is going to be a knockout."

A little dazed, Trent nodded. "It sure sounds like it."

Although Trent had seen his sister perform in several large venues, he continued to be amazed at her talent. Unlike Trent, who'd dabbled a bit here and there, Melody had embraced her musical side. As soon as she could pick up a violin, she'd started taking lessons. At eight, she'd taught herself how to play the piano and had begun composing silly little songs that her friends sang all the time, driving her two older brothers mad.

All this had ended one day when she was ten. Melody had written her first serious piece, and Trent had suggested that she record it. What was the point of having access to your very own recording studio and not using it? Trent had set up a one-hour session as a surprise for her, suspecting that if he told her in advance she'd never go through with it.

As it was, encouraged by Trent's confidence in her, she'd reluctantly agreed to record her song. She'd been struggling with the start of it when their father walked in. Or perhaps *stormed in* was a better description. Siggy had been furious at what Trent had done. He didn't want the expensive studio time wasted on his daughter. Melody had been so upset she never finished recording the song and stopped singing altogether.

From that point forward, she concentrated solely on her violin and piano, in her own way trying to please her father, just as Rafe did. Trent had gone the complete opposite direction, aggravating his father at every turn.

"Nate," Melody said from the booth, "can you play the song back so I can hear it?"

"Sure." Nate cued the song before turning to Trent. "She's such a perfectionist. I think she's recorded fifty songs."

"And I'm sure each one is better than the last. She just doesn't think she's any good. We have our father to thank for that."

Dylan was awake, his eyes bright as he listened to Melody's song. Trent unbuckled him from the stroller and lifted him so he could see his aunt. She grinned and waved. Dylan blew her a kiss and wiggled in Trent's arms.

"I've told her she has a month to whittle her album down to fourteen songs. I'm just afraid that in that time she's going to record a dozen more."

"A month? Is she planning on sticking around that long?"

"I don't know." But Nate looked troubled. "Originally I gave her two weeks, but she asked for more time."

"Is there something going on between her and Kyle?"

The way Nate's expression shut down told Trent everything he needed to know. "It's none of my business. And it's none of yours."

"She's my sister. He's my best friend."

"Stay out of it."

"Fine." He ground out the word, taking his frustration out on the wrong person.

In truth, Trent didn't want to meddle in his sister's

love life, but focusing on her distracted him from fixating on Savannah. His initial intention to keep his distance had been shattered in his office the night she'd come to Club T's. Since then, he'd involved himself in her struggles with his father and had tumbled back into her bed and under her spell.

"Melody and I agree that the album could use a duet," Nate said, unaffected by Trent's bad mood. "What would you think about recording 'She's the One' with her?"

"Me? Sing?" He preferred to make music with a guitar.

"Melody said you're pretty good."

Trent felt his face grow warm. Singing was something he enjoyed doing in the privacy of his car or shower. "I'm not professionally trained."

"You think I am? I'm just a poor kid from North Dakota who happens to like playing in a band."

Nate might be from North Dakota and he might have grown up without money, but his talent and ambition as a singer, songwriter and producer made his statement laughable.

"I'll sing," Trent said, surprising himself. "As long as you promise not to put it on the album."

"Let's record it and see how it goes."

"She'd be much better off doing a duet with you. She needs someone established to kick-start the album so she can make a pile of dough."

"You know she'd really love to put the album up for free, right?"

Trent wasn't surprised. Melody had always been

about the art, not the money. "But you talked her out of that, I hope."

"Not exactly. She's pretty adamant, and she's making enough money from touring and her songwriting royalties not to worry about a paycheck."

"But to give it away?" As a businessman, the idea pained him.

"I'll see how she feels once the whole album is done. In the meantime…" Nate leaned forward and pushed the button that would let him be heard in the recording booth. "Trent is here and he's agreed to record 'She's the One' with you."

Trent groaned as his sister's face lit up with a broad smile. "After I do this, we have some business to discuss," he said to Nate.

"Is something going on with the club?"

"Club T's is doing great. This matter is as much personal as it is business."

Nate gave him a curious look. "Does it have something to do with your sister-in-law living with you?"

Trent wasn't surprised that Nate knew about Savannah. Melody had likely mentioned that she was spending time with Dylan. "It has to do with my nephew's ownership of West Coast Records."

The two men had been friends as well as business partners for several years. Nate knew all about the family business and the difficult Siggy Caldwell.

"The shares he inherited from Rafe?"

"The company isn't doing well, and Savannah needs a large influx of cash to pay off the debt my brother stuck her with."

Nate gave a solemn nod. "Sounds like the lady needs our help. Why don't you get in there and do a little singing, and then we'll talk."

"Is Dylan okay in here with you?"

Nate took the boy and set him on his lap. "I've been dealing with temperamental artists for the last ten years. I think I can handle a one-year-old."

Grinning, Trent headed into the recording booth. The guitarist had left his instrument behind, and Trent picked it up. "Think he'd mind if I borrow this?"

"Jay's pretty cool about that sort of thing," Melody said, a half smile on her face as she watched Trent settle onto the stool and test the strings. "Are you really going to do this?"

Trent might not have been interested in a music career, but that didn't mean he couldn't have had one if he'd wanted it. Back in high school, he and a few of his buddies had formed a band and even played a few gigs. It had enhanced his bad boy mystique and got him as much action as the school's jocks. Plus, he hadn't been all banged up from playing sports.

"Nate has promised me it will never make the album," Trent said, "so I don't see what harm there is."

"We'll see." Melody gave him a sly smile. "Do you remember how it goes?"

"I think I can manage." And he started to play.

Nine

Savannah hummed as she descended in the hotel elevator, eager to head to LAX for the flight back to Las Vegas. She'd spent an eventful three days in LA and couldn't wait to get home to Dylan.

The dinner the night before at Cuts with Fred Hammer had given her a sense of what Trent was trying to provoke his father to do. It was obvious that the man knew the music business and would be a fantastic CEO for West Coast Records. The fact that he'd stolen several of the label's best artists over the last five years was a testament to his business acumen. It wasn't hard to imagine just how much it would upset Siggy to have this guy in charge of the company.

Morning sunlight poured through the lobby windows as Savannah crossed the marble floor in the direction of the exit. She was so preoccupied with thoughts of her son, she was completely caught off guard by the woman who stepped into her path.

"Savannah Caldwell."

"Yes?" She didn't recognize the brunette in snug jeans and a white T-shirt and at first thought she might have been an assistant to one of the agents she'd spoken with the day before.

The woman held out an envelope. "This is for you."

Reflexively, Savannah took it. "What is this?"

"You've been served." Without another word, the woman headed for the hotel's front entrance with the confidence of someone who had done this a thousand times before.

With her mind blank with astonishment, Savannah opened the envelope and pulled out a legal document. It didn't take her long to get the gist: contesting Rafe's bequeathing the company stock to Dylan, citing the fact that he wasn't Rafe's biological son. Every bit of optimism Savannah had gained over the last seventy-two hours vanished. Instead of leaving the hotel, she made her way to the nearest chair and dropped into it.

How was she going to explain to Trent what his father was up to? Savannah had stopped worrying about the stock and the money since she'd decided to return to acting. She would figure out a way to restructure the debt and be able to pay it off eventually. But if Trent discovered Dylan wasn't Rafe's child, he would despise her for lying to him. She needed to talk to Siggy. At least one good thing had come of this—she didn't need to fear losing her son to her father-in-law.

Savannah got in her car and headed to Siggy's house. Half of her thought she'd be denied entrance, but Siggy obviously expected her, because she was ushered right in. He was sitting behind his large desk in his office and didn't get to his feet as she entered the room.

"You're suing me?"

"I'll not have you pass off your bastard as my grandson."

Savannah resisted the urge to tell the old man that Dylan was *still* his grandson. "Dylan is Rafe's son."

"Not his biological son."

Savannah went cold. She stared Siggy down, utilizing every bit of Courtney Day she possessed to keep her panic from showing. Did he know something? Or was he guessing? She had no way of knowing without tipping her hand.

"You have no idea what you're talking about."

"I know exactly what I'm talking about. You tricked my son into marrying you and into making that boy his heir."

"That's not at all what happened." Even as she said the words, Savannah knew she was wasting her breath. "And you have no way of proving that it did."

"But I can prove that Dylan isn't Rafe's biological son. The last time he was here, I took a sample of his DNA and had it tested."

What after all this time could have prompted Siggy to do something like that? Was it because she and Trent had joined forces and were threatening his business? Her relationship with Trent while she lived in New York had never been a secret, but Siggy rarely paid attention to his son's activities. Would he have been aware that they were romantically linked? Or because he'd never viewed Savannah as being good enough to be Rafe's wife, had Siggy merely been grasping at straws?

"It doesn't matter what you can or can't prove. Rafe wanted a son and he got one."

As she spoke, Savannah began to calm down. Siggy would have a hard time contesting the will. Rafe never specified that he was leaving the stock to his biological son, and Rafe's name was on Dylan's birth certificate as his father.

"But I can drag this issue through the courts for a very long time. And when the DNA tests come back, you'll get to explain to Trent why you've been lying to him all this time." Siggy looked pleased with himself, leaving Savannah to wonder what he knew or what he thought he knew. "Meanwhile, I'll be taking back control of my company."

Now Savannah understood what Siggy was driving at. She'd helped Trent provoke his father and this was the result. And she knew Siggy was right about Trent. He'd be furious that she'd lied about Rafe being Dylan's father all this time. The only thing Savannah could do to salvage the situation was to figure out how to negotiate so Dylan's paternity never became public knowledge.

"You want your company back? I want to be out from under the debt your son created."

Siggy's eyes narrowed. "What are you offering?"

"I'll sign the stock back over to you if you'll give

me the million I owe. It's Rafe's debt, not mine, and you and I both know the stock is worth way more than that." At least until the company went under.

"If we go to court, I'll get my stock and I won't have to pay you a cent."

"Are you sure? Because if you take me to court, I'll make sure everyone knows how badly the company is doing. Including the royalties not being paid to your artists and how close you are to bankruptcy. In the meantime, I've hired Fred Hammer to take over as CEO, and his first act will be to fire Gerry and have him arrested for embezzlement. Think about it."

Leaving behind an uncharacteristically speechless Siggy, Savannah made her way out of the house. Head held high, but knees wobbling with each step, she made it to the driver's seat of her car before deflating with an enormous exhale. Determined not to break down while in sight of the house, she started the car and headed down the street. Savannah turned into the first parking lot she reached, found a vacant spot and shut off the engine.

Her forehead was halfway to the steering wheel when her phone rang, startling her. Convinced Siggy was calling to level more threats at her, Savannah was tempted not to answer. But she was a mother before anything and knew she at least had to check to see who was trying to get hold of her.

To her surprise, it was Corrine Scott, the agent she'd signed with late the previous afternoon. Corrine's offer of representation was the second one she'd received, and after spending half an hour with her, Savannah knew Corrine understood her priorities as a single mom as well as her preferences for roles.

"Hi, Corrine." With the way her day was going, Savannah braced herself for bad news. "I didn't expect to hear from you so soon."

"I didn't expect to be calling you so soon either, but when we spoke yesterday you said you were interested in looking at some movie projects. I had dinner with a producer last night and pitched you to him. He just sent over a script for a part that sounds perfect for you."

"Wow," Savannah said with a startled laugh. "You work fast." Her head was spinning from the rapid seesawing of her fortune over the last hour.

"Sometimes the perfect match between client and project takes a while—other times the stars align. I know you're flying back to Vegas, but do you have time to swing by and pick up the script to start reading?"

Savannah hadn't built in enough time for all the detours she'd encountered this morning. She closed her eyes and let her head fall back.

"I'll be by in half an hour. Would you possibly have a little time to talk about something of a personal nature? I could use an impartial point of view."

If Corrine was surprised that her new client was reaching out for some personal help, she didn't show it. "Sure. I'm happy to help any way I can."

Next, Savannah called the airline and changed her flight to later in the day, and then contacted Melody to give her the new schedule. As much as Savannah wanted to hug her baby boy, she had a legal issue and needed professional help.

Her phone rang again as she drove to Corrine's office. This time it was Trent.

"Melody said you were delayed in LA because of a project."

"I'm heading to my agent's office right now."

"Sounds like things are moving for you already."

"I'm surprised that they are. I never imagined she'd be able to find me something so fast. Of course, it's only an audition." Nevertheless, Savannah was consumed by optimism.

"What time is your flight? I'll pick you up at the airport."

"You don't need to do that."

"I have a surprise for you that won't keep."

"That sounds like trouble."

Savannah couldn't imagine what he could be up to and caught herself smiling as she ended the call. However, her delight didn't last long once her gaze fell upon the envelope containing the summons that she'd tossed onto the dashboard.

She had a tricky legal problem to deal with and if Trent learned the truth, he'd never forgive her for keeping such a huge secret from him. Which brought her thoughts back to the scene at Siggy's house. Had she really told him she'd hired Fred? And threatened to turn Gerry over to the police?

Trent was going to be unhappy with her for stomping all over his clever plan, whatever it was. He'd been cagey when she'd quizzed him about his plot to save the label. Well, if he'd wanted her to stay on script, he should have given her more information.

It was too late to worry about that now. She had a lawsuit to fight and her future to secure. On the way back to Las Vegas she would figure out what sort of explanation she should give to Trent.

Airline passengers streamed past Trent as he scanned the arrivals display to find out which carousel would contain the baggage from Savannah's flight. His timing was perfect. Her plane had touched down five minutes before. He positioned Dylan's stroller where it wouldn't be missed when Savannah came to claim their luggage.

Savannah had only been gone three days, but it felt like a lot longer. They'd spoken frequently, their exchanges revolving around Dylan and her agent while Trent's mind formed the words that would convey how much he missed her. He hadn't said any of them. His reaction to her absence disturbed him. When she'd married his brother, he'd resolved to be done with her. And for the last sixteen months, he'd believed that was the case. What a shock to discover he had been lying to himself the whole time.

The way his heart leaped when he spotted her demonstrated that he was in deeper than ever. All too aware his emotions were on display, he crouched beside the stroller and focused on unbuckling his nephew.

"Dylan, there's your mommy. Let's get you out of here so you can give her a big hug."

"Oh, I've missed you," Savannah cried, snatching Dylan into her arms and plastering noisy kisses on his cheeks. "Goodness, you've grown."

"You've only been gone three days," Trent pointed out. His arms ached to enfold her in a passionate embrace, but he shoved his hands into his pockets and welcomed her with a smile instead. "I'm sure it's impossible for him to have gotten measurably bigger in such a short period of time."

"I know." Savannah began walking in the direction of the baggage carousels. "It's just my guilt tricking me because I left him."

"He did just fine." Trent meant the words to be reassuring, but when Savannah winced, he realized he was in a no-win situation. "Even though he missed you. But Melody and I did our best to keep him entertained."

"There's no one I'd rather he spend time with than you two."

Trent decided to switch to a less emotionally charged topic. "So your trip to LA was successful. Not only did you get an agent, but also an audition for a movie role. That's great."

"It was an eventful trip. I never expected things to go so well."

"Tell me about the movie."

"It's a bigger part than I expected it to be. I skimmed through the script on the flight here. It's a romantic comedy. If I get it, I'll be the lead's best friend."

"Where is it shooting?"

The carousel began to move and the first bags appeared moments later.

"It sounds like they'll be shooting in LA." Savannah split her attention between her son and the luggage circling past them and missed Trent's frown. "I'm going back next Wednesday for the audition."

"And if you get it? Does that mean you're going back to LA?" What he wanted to know was if she was moving back permanently. Before this trip, he'd gotten the impression she wanted to make Las Vegas her home base.

"While I'm filming." She pointed to a red Tumi suitcase. "That one's mine."

Trent lifted it off the carousel while Savannah put Dylan back in his stroller. The three of them left the terminal and headed for short-term parking.

"Feels like the heat broke," Savannah commented as Trent loaded her suitcase and Dylan's stroller into the trunk of his car.

For the flight, she'd donned a sleeveless cream fit-and-flare dress with chunky gold jewelry and black-and-cream-striped pumps. The look was elegant and professional, but as she settled into the passenger seat she kicked off her high heels, unfastened her sleek updo and peeled off her jewelry. With her wavy blond hair cascading over her shoulders in luxurious disarray and her clear blue eyes sparkling as she peered at her son in the backseat, she was once again the sensual, tantalizing woman who'd haunted his dreams these last few days.

"So, I promised you a surprise," Trent said, cursing the husky rasp in his voice. He started the car's engine and turned on the stereo. The CD was ready to go—all he had to do was hit Play. "I took Dylan to the studio while Melody was recording."

Savannah's smile turned eager. "Am I finally going to hear a bit of her album?"

"It's Melody's music," he said as he backed the car out of the parking spot and headed for the exit. "But I don't think this is going to be part of her new album."

"I've been dying of curiosity for the past six hours. Are you going to play me the song or what?"

"Here goes."

He keyed the CD and waited for her reaction. Her eyes rounded with delight and she clapped her hands over her mouth. Trent found himself unable to stop grinning as the song played.

"Is that Dylan singing?"

Singing was not quite what the infant was doing, but there was no question that he was babbling all the correct notes as Melody accompanied him on the piano and sang the verses. It was one of the tunes she'd written when she was a kid, and obviously it still appealed to the under-ten-year-old set.

"Apparently they've been working on this duet since she arrived."

"It's fantastic. What a wonderful surprise. Thank you."

The song ended and Trent was about to hit the rewind button to play it again when a new song began. Nate had burned the CD for Trent. Apparently he'd decided to add a second track.

Savannah cocked her head and listened to the first strains of the new song. "I know this, don't I?"

Trent knew it all too well—it was the intro to "She's the One." He'd sung it yesterday. He had only seconds to act before it got to the part he'd recorded. "Why don't we listen to Dylan's song again."

"Wait." Savannah placed her hand over his. "That's 'She's the One.' Is Melody going to put that on her new album?"

The tension in her tone caught his attention. Glancing over, Trent noticed that Savannah's expression had grown bleak. As his sister sang the first verse, Trent wondered what about the song had caused Savannah's shift into melancholy. He was equally curious how she would react when she heard him jump in at the chorus.

"I sure hope not," he said just as his voice filled the speakers.

Hearing himself made him wince. It wasn't as if he sounded off-key or out of practice, but singing for himself and singing in the studio with his sister were meant to be private performances. Now he felt exposed. He'd been thinking about Savannah while they recorded the song, and to his sensitive ears it sounded like it.

"I had no idea." Savannah brushed back her hair with a trembling hand. She didn't finish her thought. "You guys sound great together. Melody should put it on her album."

"She needs to do a duet with someone well-known."

"You don't think anyone would remember the lead singer of Chrome Pulse?"

Trent laughed. "I sure hope not."

After a couple seconds Savannah joined him in laughing. "I can't believe Melody talked you into singing with her."

"I can't believe Nate put the song onto this CD."

Trent would definitely have some choice words for his business partner. "It wasn't meant for public consumption."

"I'm glad he did. And thank you for Dylan's song. It was really a fantastic surprise."

For a while they rode in silence, each occupied by their own thoughts. Trent wrestled with the urge to reach out and take her hand in his. Every shift in her body and subtle change in her expression caught his attention. He yearned to demonstrate how much he'd missed her. But her posture warned him that something was bothering her.

"You haven't told me much about your meeting with Fred. How did it go?"

"He's really great. I think he'd do a fantastic job running the company." She quit speaking before she ran out of air and seemed to hold the remaining breath in her lungs. It gave her statement an unfinished feel, as if she wanted to say more but decided against it.

"But?" he prompted as the silence stretched.

"I had a run-in with your father." From the way she was gripping her purse, it hadn't gone well. "I think your attempt to provoke him worked better than you thought it would."

"If he did anything to upset you…"

She blew out a shaky breath. "I might've tipped our hand about Gerry."

So that's what was bothering her.

"Why don't you start at the beginning and tell me what happened."

She took a few moments to collect her thoughts and Trent grew concerned at her reluctance.

"As I was leaving the hotel this morning, I was served with papers. Siggy is suing me for Dylan's shares in the company."

"On what grounds?"

Another long pause. "He's claiming Dylan isn't Rafe's son."

Trent tamped down irritation at his father's ridiculous tactics. "Obviously we have my father on the run, and I am glad to see that, but I'm sorry that you're the one on the receiving end of his despicable tactics. We'll get a lawyer and fight it."

"I already spoke to one today. I thought I'd better get ahead of this thing."

"Is this why you told my father that Fred would be taking over the company?"

"When I got the papers, I wasn't thinking very clearly. I stormed over to his house to confront him. I let my temper get the better of me."

Trent found this last bit rather funny. "Since when do you have a temper?"

All the times he'd stepped in and rescued her, she'd never shown any signs of being willing to fight for herself. Now that she had someone of her own to protect, she'd become more lion than mouse.

"Apparently I've grown a spine since giving birth to Dylan." The corners of her mouth lifted in a sad, ironic smile.

"You always had a spine," Trent told her, thinking about how many times she'd braved his temper after his father had gone off on him. Her only motivation had been to see if he was okay. And more often than not, he'd directed his misplaced anger at her. It had taken him years before he understood and appreciated her kindness and bravery. "You just didn't let anyone see it."

"Anyway," she said, her shoulders lifting and falling in a dismissive little shrug, "I told Siggy that I had hired Fred and intended to turn Gerry over to the police for embezzlement."

"You hired Fred?"

"I didn't. Or I hadn't at that point, anyway. But I called him later and explained the situation. He's willing to go into hostile territory and do what needs to be done. I told him it might be an interim position. Until the lawsuit is settled, everything is up in the air."

Trent blew out a breath. "You were busy."

Given all she'd accomplished, he didn't know if she needed him anymore. That bothered him more than it should. Their former dynamic gave him a mission he was comfortable with. She got into trouble. He helped her out. What role did he play in her life going forward?

"I just hope I didn't create a bigger mess."

"Whatever happens, we'll tackle it together."

Ten

Savannah considered Trent's statement in silence. When she'd explained how Siggy's lawsuit claimed Dylan wasn't Rafe's son, she'd expected Trent to grill her for answers. Instead, he perceived the legal action as a simple matter of his father playing dirty. Not for a moment had he doubted her. Savannah felt sick. Lying to Trent was eating at her. But telling him Dylan was his son would be so much worse. He'd never forgive her for deceiving him.

"I'm beginning to wonder if you shouldn't let me finish this up alone."

Trent's eyebrows went up. "You want me out just as things are getting interesting?"

"Who knows what crazy thing your father will come up with next? I don't want you hurt because of me."

"My father lost the ability to hurt me a long time ago."

Although that might be true, it didn't mean the damage had ever healed. Trent remained wary of becoming emotionally invested. And Savannah couldn't love him enough to fix what he refused to be made whole.

"That doesn't mean he won't try, and you know how he likes to play dirty."

"Trust me, when it comes to my father, I'm bulletproof."

Savannah nodded. "I should also tell you that before I spoke to a lawyer, I offered to settle with Siggy. I offered him the shares back for the million in debt I owe." When Trent shook his head, she rushed on. "I know it was foolish, but I'm sick to death of the whole thing and just want to be done."

"What did he say?"

"He told me he's going to take back the shares and not pay me a cent."

Trent nodded. "He's a pretty good poker player, and he knows you pretty well. He probably expected a bluff like that would scare you. Was this before or after you told him about Fred and Gerry?"

"Before." She didn't want to admit that she'd been scared. "His arrogance made me so mad. And after what he pulled the day I closed on my house, I don't see him as an all-powerful threat anymore."

She didn't care about the shares and she didn't care about the money. Once she was working again, she could pay off the debt she owed. The only danger she faced was if the lawsuit made public the truth about Dylan's biological father.

"Don't get between a mama and her baby."

"Darn right."

Trent laughed. The sound made Savannah smile. She was enjoying being on the same team. Being estranged from him this last year and a half had plunged her into a bleak, gray world. They might not ever be together as a family the way she wanted, but being able to laugh with him and watch him with Dylan was pretty great, too.

When the trio entered the house, Melody was in the kitchen fixing dinner while Murphy sat at her feet, his huge brown eyes luminous as he begged for handouts. Trent had given Rhoda the night off. After having her offer of help rejected, Savannah took her suitcase to the guesthouse and unpacked while Dylan sat on the bed and checked out the new puzzle she'd bought him.

Half an hour later, the four of them sat on the terrace and ate hamburgers loaded with jalapeño, guacamole and fresh tomatoes. It was a familiar family gathering. While Melody and Savannah had lived in New York City, they'd made an effort to eat together at least twice a month—more often when Trent visited.

"I really liked the duet you and Trent sang," Savannah said as talk turned to Melody's new album.

"He played that for you?" Melody shot a surprised look at her brother.

"I don't think he meant to. It was on the same CD with the song you and Dylan sang. Which was amazing, by the way." Savannah saw Trent drop a bit of hamburger to the waiting Murphy and frowned at him.

"Wasn't he great?" Melody said. "I think if the album doesn't work out I might do one for kids."

"Your album's going to be great," Trent said. "But you might think about recording your other songs, as well. I can hear kids singing about noses, roses and toeses all around the world."

"I second that," Savannah said. "So when do I get to hear more of the album?"

"She's not including the duet on her album," Trent insisted. "As a matter of fact, I'm going to get Nate to destroy the master."

"So I'll have the only copy?" Savannah rather liked the idea.

She recalled the first time she'd heard the song. Melody had written it during their days in New York. It had been a collaboration of sorts: Savannah's life put to Melody's music. Trent had never caught on that the song was about him. Originally the song had been titled "He's the One," but that had hit a little too close to home. Once Melody had changed the gender, Savannah could pretend that the lyrics were about anyone.

"Can we talk about something besides my album?" Melody said.

"Sure," Trent said, sliding a look his sister's way. "Kyle's coming into town next week. He, Nate and I are going to talk about a new business venture."

Noticing that Melody hadn't commented on Kyle's imminent arrival and was instead fussing with her nephew, Savannah picked up the conversation. "Another club?"

"Kyle wants to open one in LA. Something he can manage on a day-to-day basis." From Trent's manner, he was trying to engage his sister. Obviously Melody hadn't divulged any details about what was going on between her and Kyle. "He's been scouting properties and has narrowed it down to three."

"I'm not surprised you're looking to expand, given how well Club T's is doing."

"Of course, LA is a different market. But one that Kyle knows pretty well. He said he's been out a lot lately. I suppose it's because he's been missing you while you're on tour." This last was directed at his sister.

"It has nothing to do with me," Melody said. "Kyle's never been one to sit around for long. He likes being busy. I'm surprised it's taken this long for him to take this step. I know whenever you need him to fill in for you at Club T's he really enjoys it."

"I know he does. That's why I've asked him to stick around for the next month. I have some business in LA that's going to require me to be gone from the club quite a bit."

"He's going to stay here?" Melody didn't sound happy. "Can he do that? Take time off from his other investments, I mean."

A line formed between Trent's brows. "I thought you'd be happy to have him around while you're working on your album."

"I'll be too busy to spend time with him."

"I'm sure you can make time to be together." Trent cocked his head. "Is there something going on?"

Melody pushed back abruptly from the table, her wrought-iron chair screeching against the patio tile. "Everything is fine," she snapped, picking up her plate and heading for the kitchen.

"What the hell is going on with her?" Trent looked to Savannah for explanation. "Are she and Kyle having problems?"

"I think the tour was hard on their relationship." Savannah didn't feel bad about sharing that bit of information. It only made sense that not everyone could handle a long-distance romance. "I think it will be good for them to spend some time together here." On neutral territory.

"And it will give you and me a chance to spend some time together in LA."

"You and I? Together?" Savannah's breath caught. What was he suggesting?

"I've been thinking about it since you left. I don't feel comfortable with you and Dylan in LA by yourselves."

"If you're worried about Siggy trying to take Dylan away from me, I think his attitude on that score has changed."

"I'm not worried about my father." Trent reached over and took her hand. "I missed you these last couple days."

Savannah's throat tightened. She lowered her gaze so he wouldn't see the tears that brightened her eyes.

He'd never said anything to her like that before, and the joy she felt left her paralyzed.

"I missed you, too," she whispered, the strain on her vocal cords almost painful. "It would be nice to have you with us in LA."

"Then it's settled. Let's get this cleaned up and then I want to hear all about the movie you're going to audition for."

When they carried the dinner dishes into the kitchen, Melody chased them out before they could offer to help. "The kitchen isn't big enough for all of us."

Which wasn't at all true, but Savannah could tell Melody needed time to herself. She and Trent took Dylan to the comfortable couches in the outdoor movie theater. With the screen retracted, they enjoyed watching the sunset decorate the mountains in shades of orange and gold.

"It's beautiful here." Savannah let her head drop onto Trent's shoulder as they watched Dylan running around the open gas fireplace, currently unlit.

"Staring at that view, it's hard to believe that less than five miles away there are millions of lights and people."

"Do you ever get tired of just how crazy it is on the Strip and in the hotels? That was what drove me crazy about New York. It was always people, people and more people. I think that's why Tennessee appealed to me. Wide-open spaces where days could go by without seeing anyone."

"That's why I bought this place. To get away from it all."

"You do have your own little vacation spot here."

"Do you really want to go back to LA? The traffic? Everyone on top of one another?"

"If I want to get jobs, I'm pretty sure that's where I need to be."

"Scarlett makes it work, going back and forth."

"She has two careers and a husband who lives here." Savannah hadn't meant to imply anything by this last remark. Nevertheless, she felt Trent stiffen. Containing a weary sigh, Savannah patted him on his knee and got to her feet. "It's past Dylan's bedtime."

She expected Trent to be happy to escape after the direction the conversation had gone, but he surprised her by dogging her steps to the guesthouse. When she gave him a questioning look, he shrugged.

"I've been reading Dylan a bedtime story. I know it's something you do for him every night, so I thought he'd expect it."

Once again Trent had taken her by surprise. "That's nice, but I've got this."

"Sounds like you're trying to get rid of me."

"Not at all." But suddenly she understood a bit of what Melody was feeling. Keeping disappointment or upset hidden wasn't easy. But the last thing she wanted to do was talk about how she was feeling and have it end in an argument. "I just thought maybe you'd be tired of babysitting."

Savannah entered Dylan's room and began pulling out what she needed to get him ready for bed. Trent demonstrated just how much time he'd been spending with Dylan as he made himself useful, gathering diapers and baby wipes.

"We still haven't talked about the movie," he said, spreading a changing pad on the bed.

Savannah laid Dylan down and began stripping off his clothes. "We can talk about it tomorrow."

"You are trying to get rid of me."

She didn't answer right away but kept her hands busy and her attention focused on her son. But their nighttime routine of tickling and giggling couldn't distract her from the tall man standing beside her, observing their antics. At last all the snaps on his pajamas were closed and her son was ready for bed.

"Who's ready for bed?" she crooned, making her son smile. His upper teeth were starting to come in, and she was struck by how fast he was growing up. Overcome by a rush of sentimentality, she lifted him into her arms and snuggled him against her chest, but to her shock, he reached out to Trent.

"I think he wants me to read him a story."

Flabbergasted, Savannah turned her son over to Trent. He settled with Dylan in the chair and pulled out a board book. While Savannah watched her two favorite men, Trent read one book after another until he had gone through Dylan's library.

"That's enough reading for one night," Savannah said, her tone firm.

She picked up her sleepy son and settled him in his crib with his favorite toy. She turned on the lamp that threw dancing shadows on the ceiling and then headed to the door. With one last glance at the crib, she turned off the overhead light.

"Are you okay?" Trent asked as they made their way into the living room.

"Fine. Why wouldn't I be?"

"You and Dylan have been alone for a long time. With so many of us taking care of him now, I thought you might miss having him all to yourself."

He'd captured a little of what she was feeling. "Not at all. I'm thrilled that he has so many people in his life who love him."

What bothered her was how attached Trent had become to Dylan. It made her all the more conflicted about not telling him that Dylan was his son. While she'd watched Trent reading the silly stories Dylan loved so much, she'd been consumed by guilt. All the time she'd kept the two of them apart, never imagining Trent had any interest in children.

Trent took her hand and guided it to his cheek. Her other hand he pulled around his waist. Held close, she inhaled the comforting masculine scent of him and her pulse danced. She could get used to coming home to Trent. When he'd visited her in New York, she'd rushed back to her apartment and fallen into his arms after a long day of shooting.

But those moments, wonderful though they were, had been short-lived. Trent might enjoy a week or two of domestic bliss, but he grew restless soon after. Having her and Dylan stay with him was a novelty. Soon enough they'd be in his way. She wanted to be gone before that happened.

"On the way back from LA, I did some thinking."

"Tell me later."

Before she could protest, his mouth found hers and she was lost in the sweeping power of his kiss. What good was it to fight the magic between them? In the future, she would have months and years to ache for him. Today, she intended to take whatever he would give her.

Trent didn't know why this particular Friday night at the club was driving him crazy. It wasn't as if more things than usual were going wrong. At the moment he was staring at his most experienced waitress. She'd messed up the tab for one of their biggest VIPs. Trent had to decide whether to eat the twenty-thousand-dollar mistake and keep the client happy or risk pissing off someone who had been known to drop upward of three hundred grand in the club when he was in town.

"Give this to Jason and tell him not to bother Khalid." Trent signed off on the report she brought to him about the discrepancy and handed it over.

"I'm really sorry, Trent."

"Figure out what happened and get it fixed."

Gina nodded and raced away. Trent watched her go with more than a trace of impatience. Normally he wouldn't be this short with his staff even over a mistake of this size, but Savannah had been in LA for four days and this time she'd taken Dylan with her. Dammit, he missed her. He missed both of them.

"So this is where you're hiding." Kyle Tailor entered Trent's office, his long legs carrying him across the room in four strides. "I've been looking all over the club for you. The place is packed."

"When did you get in?"

"Half an hour ago. I came here straight from the airport."

Trent was wondering why his best friend had chosen to visit Club T's over reuniting with the woman he loved first. "Are you meeting Melody here?"

"No, it's late. I'll see her tomorrow."

"I'm sure she'd like to see you tonight."

"I really don't want to bother her."

"Bother her?" Trent stared at his friend in dismay. "I was right. There is trouble between you two. Is it because she was on tour for so long?"

"What has she said?"

"Nothing. And that's what's weird. Normally she talks about you all the time. It's kind of annoying."

"Well, maybe that's because she's not in love with me anymore."

"Has she said that?"

"Not in so many words."

"Then what are you basing it on?" Trent waited for his friend's reply. When Kyle kept his lips pressed together, a belligerent scowl pulling down his brows, Trent said, "I know my sister. If she wasn't in love with you, she'd let you know." Still, Kyle said nothing. "Did you do something?"

"What makes you think it's my fault?"

Disgusted, Trent shook his head. "Because she's down in the dumps and you sound defensive."

"Can we not talk about your sister? I'm here to

have some fun. Let's grab some drinks and find some women who want to have a good time."

Trent couldn't believe what his best friend was saying. They'd just been talking about the problems he and Melody were having and Kyle wanted to chase women? But when he took a harder look at Kyle, Trent recognized the desperate edge in his friend's expression. As if he intended to have fun even if he didn't feel like it. Deciding Kyle wasn't as indifferent to his problems with Melody as he was trying to appear, Trent swallowed the harsh lecture he'd been about to deliver.

"I can't right now," Trent said. "It's been a crazy night, with one thing after another going wrong." Almost as if on cue, Trent's phone buzzed, delivering another text message. Now they were running out of a particular vodka that one of their VIPs preferred. He exhaled and got to his feet. "To top it off, our DJ got sick at the last minute, so I've got Nate up on stage."

"I saw. The crowd seems to be enjoying him a lot."

"You know, for an introvert, he's a pretty decent showman."

They both laughed. Few people would characterize the front man for Free Fall as an introvert, but in truth, as much as he enjoyed making music, Nate needed a lot of downtime during his tours.

"Come on," Trent said, heading for the door. "Why don't you come with me while I put out a couple fires, and then I'll show you some of the upgrades we've done to the outside since you were last here."

Kyle grumbled about coming to Vegas to play, not work, but he accompanied Trent on his rounds. To

Trent's surprise, his friend stuck with him the whole night, even though he had several offers to hang out with some very beautiful women. They parted ways at three. Kyle was heading off to try his luck at the tables and Trent still had work to do.

At five he debated the feasibility of heading home for a couple hours. He had a meeting with a new liquor distributor at eight. If he stayed on his couch, he could catch an extra hour of sleep. But as he lay staring at the shadowy ceiling, his overactive mind kept him awake.

He was back to thinking about Kyle and Melody. Although Trent had been opposed to their relationship when he'd originally learned of it, he'd come around after seeing how happy his sister was with Kyle. Now, however, he was worried that Melody was going to get hurt, and he knew she would be furious with him if he interfered.

A few hours later, the meeting with his potential distributor went well. Trent had managed to catch enough sleep to give the guy a fair hearing. The addition of some unique, high-end product would enhance the appeal of Club T's in an already cutthroat market. The club's closest competitor might be seven million a year behind them in sales, but that could change if Club T's had a couple bad months.

Eager to catch a few more hours of sleep, Trent headed home. The smell of coffee hit him as he entered his open-concept living space from the garage. He sucked in a big breath and felt revitalized. All thoughts of heading off to bed vanished as he spied Savannah and Dylan out on the terrace. She was sitting on the concrete while Dylan put a ball through a miniature basketball hoop.

Leaving his tie and suit coat draped over the banister, Trent poured himself a cup of coffee and headed out to enjoy the cool morning.

Savannah glanced his way as he approached. "Are you just getting home?"

"It was a late night and I had a meeting at eight this morning." He sat in the chair nearest the pair and sipped from his mug. Murphy came over to greet him, and Trent lifted the Frenchie onto his lap and gave him a thorough scratching. The dog snorted with pleasure. "I grabbed a couple hours' sleep on the couch in the office."

She acknowledged his statement with a nod and arced the ball through the hoop. Given the size of the target and her distance of five feet, it was an impressive toss.

"Score," she called, raising her arms, and Dylan mimicked her.

Despite her obvious pleasure in watching her son, Savannah seemed quieter than normal. Trent noticed that although her lips curved in a smile, her eyes never lit up. Given her friendship with Melody and the fact that Kyle's car wasn't parked in the driveway, Trent suspected she was worried about his sister.

"Is something wrong?" Trent asked, not wanting to come straight out with his own concerns until he knew which way the wind blew.

"My lawyer called a little bit ago and told me your father's backing down on the lawsuit." Savannah's gaze tracked Dylan as he chased his ball along the terrace. "Not only that, but he's offering to pay me one point five million for Dylan's shares."

Given her somber mood, this wasn't at all what he'd been expecting. "That's not even close to what those shares are worth."

"I know, but it's enough to pay off Rafe's debts and give me a nest egg."

"You should counter."

Savannah looked horrified at his suggestion. "I'm just relieved to have it all done."

So why didn't she look as if things were going her way? More than anything Trent wanted her to be happy. His father had caused her enough harm. And should have to pay.

"Do you have any idea what caused him to change his mind?" Trent asked.

"No, and my lawyer also questioned his abrupt turn-around, as well. He did a little investigating and discovered someone wants to buy West Coast Records."

"So there's a chance for you to make even more money."

"And a chance for Siggy to ruin the whole thing."

"So you've made up your mind." He set the dog back on the ground and watched him run over to Dylan.

"I've already given the go-ahead to sell the shares back to Siggy."

"Then why aren't you celebrating?"

"I should be. It's stupid that I'm not."

Trent was starting to understand. "You wish you'd

been able to fight him to get what the shares were worth."

"No, I'm happy with our deal the way it stands. I didn't marry Rafe for his money. I married him to give Dylan a traditional family. Now that Rafe is dead, I have accepted that Dylan and I will be fine on our own."

It wasn't the first time Trent was filled with admiration for her. The girl he'd grown up with, the woman he'd known in New York, hadn't been confident and strong. Savannah might still need help from time to time, but she didn't need rescuing. She'd stood up to his father and participated in Trent's scheme to provoke his father into acting. She might not have anticipated what Siggy would do, but she'd taken charge when he threatened her with a lawsuit.

"So what is really going on?"

Her big blue eyes turned sorrowful. "There's something I should've let you know a long time ago."

Anxiety twisted his gut at the pained expression on her face. "Like what?"

"It has to do with your father's lawsuit. He claimed Dylan isn't Rafe's son." She clenched her fists and leaned forward. "It's true."

Trent's thoughts froze. Once again his perception of her changed. "So that's why you chose not to fight him? Because you knew you'd lose?"

"No. I meant what I said about the money. I only wanted what's fair."

"Did Rafe know Dylan wasn't his son?" For the first time since he'd found out that Rafe and Savannah were getting married, Trent felt sorry for his brother. "Or did you lie to him, too?"

Hurt flickered in her eyes, but she didn't let her chin droop. "Rafe knew before he proposed to me. At the time I didn't understand why he would want to raise a son who wasn't biologically his. I didn't realize it at the time, but the cancer treatments had made him sterile. Your father had drilled the concept of dynasty into Rafe's head for so long that even as he was dying, he was determined to make Siggy happy."

"So you both lied to my father."

"Yes. At the time I was in a vulnerable place—pregnant and terrified of raising Dylan alone." She didn't need to add that Rafe had been there to pick up the pieces after she and Trent had broken up.

"That first night in my office, when you told me Dylan was Rafe's son." Trent wasn't sure he recognized the woman standing before him. "You were lying."

She shook her head. "As far as Rafe was concerned, Dylan was his son. But he wasn't his biological child."

Never before had he perceived Savannah as being duplicitous. But she'd lied to him and to his family. Could she also be lying about Rafe knowing that Dylan wasn't his?

"Is lack of money for a long, drawn-out legal case the reason you're no longer fighting Siggy for Dylan's right to the stock? Or are you suffering a guilty conscience?"

"Will you condemn me if I tell you it's a little of both?"

Trent held perfectly still and stared at her. A question was burning a hole in his heart. Who was Dylan's father? He thought he knew Savannah inside and out. Had she had a fling or a one-night stand? The thought disturbed him.

"I never in a million years thought you'd do something like this." His voice sounded flat and wooden.

"Like what?"

"Pass a stranger's child off as Rafe's."

"I didn't. Don't you understand?" Savannah released a long-suffering sigh at his head shake. "He has your smile."

"Who does?" Trent had no idea what she was getting at.

"Dylan."

What was she trying to say? Trent stared at her, his mind blank.

Savannah looked miserable. She'd obviously been expecting a different reaction. "Trent, Dylan is your son."

Eleven

Funny how easily the confession slipped free. She'd been dreading this moment since the pregnancy test had come back positive. But in the end it wasn't as traumatic as she thought it was going to be. She'd already lost her self-respect and her uncomplicated future to the lie. Trent's confession that he'd not wanted their relationship to end had cut deep. What if instead of being afraid to be rejected she'd gone to him when she first found out she was pregnant? Her life might have turned out very differently.

"That's impossible," Trent said. "We were always very careful."

"This is going to sound crazy." Savannah braced to defend herself, suspecting Trent would be skeptical of her convoluted explanation. "When I came to visit you in Vegas that last time, I did so on Rafe's recommendation."

"Rafe told you to come see me?"

"As I was getting settled in LA, he and I began to spend time together. He said he'd been in love with me a long time and wanted us to be together. I liked Rafe, but he knew I loved you."

"If he wanted you, wouldn't it make more sense for him to keep you away from me?"

"Yes, if he'd actually loved me. But as I found out after we got married, he was merely using me." She studied Trent's face and saw only confusion and doubt. "And using you."

"Using us how?"

"He needed an heir. He wanted one who looked like a Caldwell." She raised her eyebrows and stared at him, waiting for him to understand what she was saying.

"But we were careful," he repeated.

"That last time we were together…the condoms we used… Rafe gave me those condoms and told me to get you out of my system."

"Seriously?" Trent looked completely shell-shocked. And angry. "You didn't think that was strange?"

"Maybe." She thought back to how desperate and miserable she'd been at the time. "I thought he was trying to be helpful. I never imagined he'd do something as crazy as sabotage the condoms."

"He *wanted* you to get pregnant? To what end?"

"So that there'd be a Caldwell to eventually take over at West Coast Records."

"Do you hear how insane that sounds?"

"I've been living with this for the last year and a half." Savannah's strength was draining. She crumpled into a nearby chair and put her hands in her lap. "I was the one he duped. How do you think I feel?"

"You don't think we're both victims in this?"

Trent paced away toward the terrace and stood with his back to her. He remained as still as a statue for a long time until he finally asked, "Were you ever planning on informing me Dylan is my son?"

She should have been better prepared for this question. As it was, she'd spent all her time worrying about what the fallout for her and Dylan would be if—when—Trent learned the truth.

"To what end?" Her response might have been harsh, but Trent had made his opinion clear. "You never wanted to be part of a family. Rafe did."

"You had no right making that decision for me." Trent turned to face her. His expression was bleak.

Remembering how that final conversation with him had gone, Savannah hardened her heart. "That last morning we were together, you told me you had no time or energy for anything but the club."

"And at that particular moment I didn't. We'd been open barely six months and every day there was something new going wrong. We'd made a huge investment and in order to make it pay off, I had to give it a hundred and ten percent."

"I heard that loud and clear. You didn't have time for me. Why would I think you would have time for me and our child?"

"You should have told me," he insisted.

Savannah refused to regret the decision she'd made. Loving Trent had led to heartache. Marrying Rafe had seemed a safe and sensible alternative.

"You know now," she said, her strength returning as she settled on a course of action. Savannah got to her feet and headed toward him. "You have a son, Trent. What do you intend to do about it?"

She'd never challenged him directly before. Her question was born of frustration and longing. More than anything she needed him to step up and demand to be in Dylan's life. To be part of her life.

"Honestly, I don't know." He raked his hand through his hair. "I need some time to think."

She barely registered the disappointment that washed through her. His answer didn't surprise her at all. "You know, nothing about your life needs to change the least bit," she told him. "Something's going to break for me in LA. In fact, I just found out I have to head back there tomorrow."

"Already?"

"My agent is excited about my acting prospects. She was able to line up another audition. It looks like my future is there."

Maybe she'd look for a rental. It hurt to give up her plans for buying a house in Las Vegas and living near Trent, but he didn't appear as if he was going to step up and be Dylan's father.

"Your future?" he echoed. "You're not going to stay in Las Vegas?"

The question gave her the opening she needed to ask what was burning in her heart. "Do you want us to stay? Dylan needs a father. I…" She sucked in a breath for strength before putting it all out there. "I need you. I always have."

Trent's features turned to stone. "You can't expect—"

"No." Between one heartbeat and the next, Savannah embraced Courtney Day. The character gave her the dignity to speak mildly and conceal her anguish. "I don't expect. And that's why I'm leaving. Moving to LA is practical. I'll be closer for auditions and meetings." When Trent didn't say anything, Savannah rushed on. "I need to pack. I'll be by later to say goodbye."

And before she was overwhelmed by the sobs tearing at her throat, she left him.

Outrage consumed Trent as he watched Savannah pick Dylan up and walk away with her head held at a defiant angle. He couldn't get past how many times she had looked him in the eye and let him believe Dylan was Rafe's son. And then today she'd acted as if by keeping the truth hidden she'd done him some sort of favor.

Realizing his hands were clenched into fists, Trent shook his arms to release the tension. But nothing could unravel the knot in his chest. He headed for his room and grabbed a quick shower. There was no way he was going to be able to sleep, so he headed back to the club.

In the months following his breakup with Savannah, Trent had thrown himself into making Club T's into the go-to spot on the Strip. Besides having a killer lineup of DJs, he was constantly looking at ways to improve service and ambience. He had a list of things he wanted to upgrade, including the lighting and sound.

When he got to his office, he was surprised to find Kyle there.

"Where have you been?" Trent asked. If he asked a little more forcefully than he needed to, it was due to his concern for Melody. "I expected to see you at the house. Tell me you didn't hook up with somebody."

"Nothing like that." Kyle didn't overreact to Trent's aggressive tone or nosiness. "I took a suite here at the hotel."

"Why aren't you staying at the house? Have you called Melody? What the hell is going on with you two?" Trent knew he wasn't giving his friend a chance to answer, but his own troublesome morning had put him on edge.

"Look, I didn't say anything last night, but we've had a rough patch."

"How rough?"

Kyle's expression darkened. "I'm here, aren't I? In Vegas, I mean. And at Cobalt. I don't know what's going on at the moment."

He looked utterly miserable, so Trent decided to cut him some slack.

"So what brings you here this morning?"

"You got your start in the LA club scene. I know they make a tenth of what we bring in at Club T's. Do you think it makes sense for us to open something in LA?"

"I'm looking at some other business opportunities in LA," Trent said, thinking about Savannah and the rebirth of her acting career. Of course, when he'd started considering ventures that would take him to LA and into her orbit, he hadn't known she'd been keeping his son from him for a year. "I thought I would explore expanding into LA."

"Great. I talked with Nate for a while last night and he's on board, as well." Kyle crossed the office to the window that overlooked the club. "He told me that you have Savannah staying with you. Are you sure that's a good idea?"

"I'm just helping her out for old times' sake. She and Siggy have been at odds over the label and he's been playing dirty."

Kyle gave a rough laugh. "Just like old times, then."

"Just like."

"I found out something just now." Trent had no idea he was going to share Savannah's revelation until the words came out of his mouth. "Savannah told me Dylan is my son."

"She cheated on Rafe with you?"

Trent had no idea why Kyle had leaped to that conclusion. "No, she married him after finding out she was pregnant with Dylan."

"She never told you she was pregnant?" Kyle looked appalled. "That's messed up."

Hearing his own opinion echoed by his best friend, Trent began to feel a little vindicated. "She should've come to me."

"Absolutely. Your poor brother."

"Rafe knew. Apparently his cancer had made him

infertile. He was glad to be a father and have a son to pass the business along to."

Trent felt at that moment that he understood what his brother had been up against. Maybe setting up Savannah to get pregnant had been a crazy act, but with the cancer eating away at his mind, no doubt he hadn't been thinking rationally.

"What would you have done if she'd told you before marrying Rafe?"

This was a question Trent should have asked himself already, but he'd been so consumed with anger at being lied to. "I don't know. Obviously I would have taken care of her and the baby." Taken care of her financially was what he meant to say.

"But would you have married her? I know how you feel about getting tied down, but you've been crazy about Savannah for a long time."

"Maybe." *Probably not.* "We'll never know." Funny how twenty-four hours earlier he'd been thinking how great things were between them and how much he was enjoying having Dylan around.

"So that's it then? You guys are done?"

Were they done? Of course they were. A bone-deep chill struck Trent.

"She's planning on restarting her acting career." He sounded calm and detached. Numb. "That means she's going to be spending time in LA."

"How much time?"

He had to think about their last conversation. "Probably full time."

And just like that it hit him. Savannah wasn't going

to be back and forth between Las Vegas and LA like she'd first talked about doing.

She was leaving and taking Dylan. His son. Trent was still reeling from the knowledge that he was a father. Now it occurred to him that he and Dylan were going to be very far apart.

"How are you going to see Dylan if they're living there? I mean, if it was my kid, I'd never want to be away from him."

Kyle had made a good point. Did Savannah expect that Trent would just give up his son? "I haven't really thought the whole thing through."

"You should talk to her about sharing custody."

"I don't know if she'd be open to that."

"You could demand it."

Trent recoiled from Kyle's suggestion. He was sick of being at odds with Savannah. Until recently he hadn't been able to admit how his world had been disrupted when he'd lost her.

"I'll think about it."

"I don't envy you," Kyle said. "When the kids come into the picture, it messes everything up."

With that said, Trent changed the subject. The two men talked business for a couple hours before grabbing lunch. Then they went to Nate's studio and brought him up to speed. By the time Trent returned to his house at three, he was fighting the drag of exhaustion from his sleepless nights.

Unfortunately any hope of a catnap before he headed back to the club was shattered when he opened up the door between the garage and the house and discovered his houseguests in high spirits. Their excited voices reached his ears and raked across his raw nerves before he stepped across the threshold. On the edge since he left the house earlier that day, Trent felt a snarl form on his lips.

"What's going on?" he demanded, eyeing the open bottle of sparkling grape juice on his breakfast bar and the almost-empty flutes.

"We're celebrating," Melody said. "Savannah just found out she got the movie."

Trent should've been happy for her, but he hadn't gotten over what he'd learned that morning. "You must be thrilled."

If she noticed that he was less than enthusiastic, she didn't react. "I'm more nervous than anything else."

"You don't have to be," he said, mood softening as he noticed her uncertainty. "You're going to be great." He remembered watching her on the set of *Loving New York*. She'd been confident and professional. Before that, he'd been accustomed to thinking of her as a naive girl. The transformation to accomplished actress had forced him to reevaluate who she was. "When do you start filming?"

"Next month, but they want me next week for wardrobe." She looked dazed by all the sudden changes.

He understood how she was feeling. He was off balance, as well.

"How long is shooting supposed to take?" Melody asked.

"I was told to expect ten to twelve weeks."

"You're going to need a place to stay," Melody said.

"I have a friend who might be able to help you with that."

"Actually, I've already found a small house to rent for the next six months."

"Sounds like everything's working out." Trent tasted bitter disappointment at how fast everything had been arranged. He wasn't prepared for her to leave him and take Dylan away. His gut twisted and sweat beaded on his skin.

The conversation with Kyle rose in his thoughts. Should he demand partial custody? But was that really what he wanted? For his son to be shuttled back and forth between Las Vegas and LA?

Savannah didn't look at him as she said, "Dylan and I have imposed on you long enough. We'll be out of your hair tomorrow."

"That's not how I feel about having you here." But the words lacked sincerity.

She'd lied to him, and he couldn't get past that. Even so, her expectant expression tore at him. She was waiting for him to say something heartfelt and romantic. Maybe that he wanted them to stay. That he couldn't live without her or their son.

But so much was wrong between them and anger was a familiar, uncomplicated emotion. He held on to it even as concern over losing her and Dylan gnawed at him.

"Nevertheless, it's time we start the next chapter of our life." Savannah glanced at her son as he yawned. "Looks like someone's ready for his nap. I'd better go put him down."

Savannah had barely stepped out onto the terrace when Melody rounded on Trent.

"You're not really going to let her move to LA, are you?"

"She has a part in a movie that's filming there. I don't know why you think I'd stop her."

"I'm probably the last person to be giving romantic advice, but you two belong together. I've known it since those days in New York. I know it upset you when she married Rafe." Melody held up her hand to forestall the denial that leaped to his lips. "Don't even try to deny it. I saw you at the wedding."

"Sometimes it doesn't work between people."

"Sometimes people are unwilling to work at it."

"Are we talking about Savannah and me? Or you and Kyle?"

"All four of us, I think."

"So what are you going to do about it?"

"This isn't about me. This is about you. You are about to let go of the only woman you've ever loved. And why?"

"She lied to me. She's been lying to all of us. Dylan is my son."

"Yikes." Melody grimaced but didn't look surprised. "She finally told you."

"You knew?"

"Since the day before she married Rafe. She was having serious doubts about going through with the wedding. I told her to follow her heart. I thought that meant she would tell you about the baby."

"But she didn't." Trent remembered how he'd expected her to call off the wedding right up until the moment she actually said, "I do." He'd left right after the ceremony and never congratulated her or his brother. "Obviously she found what she needed in Rafe."

"In some ways, I think she did. You should've seen her that morning. She was a wreck. Pacing. Hyperventilating. I thought for sure she was going to call it off. And then Rafe came in." Melody's eyes took on a faraway look. "He sat her down and knelt before her. He took her hand in his and very calmly convinced her that he would make sure everything was going to be all right." Melody blinked back tears. "None of us knew that he wouldn't be around to fulfill that promise."

A complicated mix of emotions churned in Trent's gut. He'd loved his brother and resented him in equal measure. He'd learned that Rafe had betrayed him, but he also had to acknowledge that by marrying Savannah, Rafe had tried to take care of her the way Trent had refused to.

He didn't want to think about Rafe being a good guy. It was easier to dwell on all the things he'd done wrong. And yet without Rafe, there would be no Dylan and Trent might never have had a second chance with Savannah.

A second chance that had ended as badly as the first one.

"I wonder," Melody continued, "after all this time, Savannah changed her mind about telling you the truth."

"Siggy was suing her for the shares in the company Rafe left Dylan. He was claiming Dylan wasn't Rafe's son. I think she expected the truth to come out. So she let me know."

"Are you sure that's why? Maybe she hoped once you knew Dylan was your son that you might ask her to stay. She still loves you. I just know it."

"That's not the way it seems to me."

Savannah had given up her dream of a blissful, traditional family with him. She'd decided being Dylan's mom was enough. And for some strange reason that angered Trent more than all the rest put together.

"Is this really what you want?" Melody demanded, irritation snapping in her voice.

For the last twelve hours, Trent had been too preoccupied by how he'd been wronged by the people who should have his back to give much thought to what he wanted.

"What do you mean?"

"Do you really want to live here alone while your son and the woman you love live in a different state?"

"The woman I love?" He gave a bitter laugh, wishing he'd kept his distance from Savannah the way he had for the last year and a half. "What I want is to take back the last two weeks."

"You don't mean that."

"I do. I wish Savannah had never come to Vegas to ask me for help. Because if she hadn't, I'd never have learned the truth."

On the terrace edge, out of sight of the living room's occupants, Savannah heard Trent's declaration and felt neither shock nor hurt. In fact, she was a little relieved.

Now she didn't have to wonder if returning to LA was the right decision. Trent didn't want her or Dylan in his life. She could stop looking back and move forward.

Savannah entered the guesthouse and closed the sliding glass doors to the patio. With her bags packed and her flight several hours away, she kept herself busy cleaning the bathroom and little-used kitchen until Dylan woke.

Feeling restless and needing to get away from the house, Savannah took Dylan to the nearby mall and window-shopped for a couple hours. She kept melancholy at bay by thinking about what homey touches would warm up the cute mission-style house she'd rented. By the time she returned to Trent's house, it was close to six and she knew he would have left for the club.

Melody's car was gone as well and Savannah was able to relax knowing she wouldn't run into either of them. She set about heating up the leftover chicken she'd fixed for dinner the night before. Dylan was a good eater. He scarfed down the chunks of carrots and potato as well as the bits of thigh meat Savannah arranged on the high-chair tray.

Later, Savannah sat with Dylan on the couch and read to him, losing herself in the rhythm of the words and her son's delight. When she ran out of books, she turned to her phone and the playlist that contained all his favorite songs. He laughed and clapped his hands while she sang. For a while longer she was able to escape her sadness. And then she heard the first few notes of the song Dylan and Melody had recorded. Days earlier, she'd uploaded the song, and now she played it for him often. His ability to mimic the tune amazed her. Before she could hit the repeat button, the other song from the CD began to play.

Savannah's finger hovered over the stop button. Dwelling on her foolish dreams wasn't conducive to moving forward. But the magic of Melody's lyrics being sung in Trent's deep voice was hard to resist. She didn't realize she was crying until she noticed that Dylan was watching her with solemn eyes. He put his palms on her wet cheeks. With a shaky laugh, she kissed his damp fingers and dashed the remaining moisture from her skin.

"Mommy's being silly, isn't she?" The last strains of "She's the One" faded and the room grew silent. Needing a distraction, Savannah got to her feet. With Halloween a week away, she'd bought Dylan a costume but hadn't yet tried it on him. "You're going to be the cutest dragon LA has ever seen," she promised as she slipped his chubby thighs into the blue-and-green suit with orange wings and spikes down the tail.

Once she had the zipper up and the hood lifted into place, she started working on his roar. He was slowly learning his animal sounds and mastered the dragon's growl after a few minutes. Laughing at the cuteness overload, she spun with Dylan in her arms and he shrieked with delight.

Why had she once worried so much about being a part of a traditional family with Trent when what she should have wished for was a perfect family? Because somehow that's the exact sort of family she'd become with Dylan. Perfect.

Twelve

Club T's throbbed with ear-blasting electronic music and pulsed with a dazzling light display. Trent sat in his favorite spot and watched the crowd drink and dance, laugh and flirt. A stunning blonde sat to his right. He'd forgotten her name as soon as they'd been introduced. She was a friend of the redhead Kyle had plucked out of the crowd waiting behind the velvet ropes.

Trent's cell phone buzzed with an incoming text from Nate.

You don't look like you're having fun.

He glared over to where Nate sat on the far end of the curved couch, his lips twisted in a sardonic smile.

The club was too noisy for conversation to carry over that distance, so Trent texted back.

I'm working.

Nate checked the incoming message and responded without looking up.

Kyle and I have this. Maybe you should get out of town for a few days.

Where the hell was he supposed to go? He rejected the first idea that popped into his head. Going to LA to check out the potential club properties Kyle had scouted would put him too near Savannah and Dylan. He wasn't ready to deal with that situation yet. His emotions were too raw.

Amid the loud music in the club, Trent reflected on the playful growls and unrestrained laughter that had drifted across his quiet backyard the other night. He'd been standing on his terrace, overlooking his pool when the sounds had first caught his attention. Drawn by the joyful noise, he'd crossed half the distance to the guesthouse before reality had caught up with him. Unfortunately, although he'd stopped himself from joining them, it had taken him ten minutes to turn away. The memory of how he'd ached standing there alone in the dark compressed his lungs.

He would head to New York City and put the entire country between him and Savannah. Visiting his mother would take his mind off his troubles. She was directing her first off-Broadway musical and had been pestering him for months to fly out and see it. He texted Nate back.

Sounds good.

Figuring he might as well get started immediately, Trent left the couch, shaking off the blonde woman who'd clutched at his jacket sleeve. He hadn't consumed more than a single scotch, but as he made his way out of the club, he felt disconnected from his environment, as if he'd overindulged.

Six hours later he checked into his hotel in Times Square and ordered breakfast from room service. By the time he ate and showered, it was late enough that he could call his mother without waking her.

"You're in New York City?" At eight in the morning, she sounded wide-awake and delighted to hear he was in town.

"I came in a few hours ago. Kyle and Nate are both in Las Vegas, so I thought I'd take some time off and come visit you."

"I'm so glad. I have to be at the theater at ten. We're making some minor changes to one of the scenes." The play had opened a week before to mixed but mostly positive reviews. His mother was a perfectionist, always taking her craft up a notch. "You can take me to lunch and tell me all of what's going on in your life."

"I'll be there."

Trent hung up and headed for the lobby. His favorite thing to do when he came to New York was to walk the streets and absorb the energy. The city's pace was just as hectic as Las Vegas's, but here people moved with purpose, the vibe oriented toward both business and artistic pursuits.

At five minutes before ten, he met his mother on the sidewalk in front of the theater. She wore a long gray sweater belted over black leggings and a slouchy black trench coat. Bright red lipstick emphasized her broad smile. These days she was always happy. It hadn't been that way when he was young. Sometimes when Siggy hadn't been home she would sing with Trent and Melody, but even then her eyes had carried shadows.

"How wonderful to see you." His mother trapped his face between her hands and brought his head down so she could kiss his cheek. Then she peered at him. "You look tired."

"I flew the red-eye and didn't sleep."

"With all the crazy hours you work at that club of yours, I would think you'd be used to it." She linked her arm through his and drew him into the theater. "I hear Melody's back in the studio. Is she ever going to finish her album?"

"Nate has given her a deadline and threatened to pick the songs himself if she doesn't start making some decisions."

"Is she happy?"

Trent gave his mother's question serious consideration. It wouldn't do to fire off a hasty answer. "Yes and no."

"Why, yes?"

"I think she's glad to be done with the tour. The traveling and performing are not her cup of tea. And she's having fun playing in the studio. It's what she loves.

It wouldn't surprise me if one day she stopped singing and went into production full-time."

"It's too bad Siggy can't appreciate musical genius. She would've been a great asset to West Coast Records." His mother slipped off her coat and draped it over her arm. "So would you."

Trent shrugged. He'd given up on pleasing his father before he'd become a teenager. "Siggy didn't want me within a mile of his company, and he only sees Melody as a little girl."

Naomi shook her head. "So why is my daughter unhappy?"

"I don't know for sure, because neither of them is confiding in me, but I think Melody and Kyle are having problems. Right now they are both in Las Vegas, but from what I can tell they haven't seen each other yet."

"That's the feeling I get, as well," his mother said, her sigh speaking volumes. "She stopped talking about him three months ago. I think something happened when she broke from the tour to visit him in LA."

"They'll figure it out."

His mother regarded Trent with surprise. "That's very optimistic of you."

"You don't think I'm right?"

"No, I think you're right." Her eyes narrowed and she seemed to be searching for something in his expression. "I'm just surprised that your opinion is so upbeat."

"I don't understand what you mean."

"You aren't exactly a believer when it comes to romance and relationships. Do you remember saying that your brother's marriage wouldn't last a year?"

And it hadn't. Just not for the reason Trent had thought.

"I didn't think Rafe and Savannah were meant for each other."

"Because she was your girlfriend first?"

Two years ago he'd never imagined he would lose her. By the time he figured out that he didn't want to live without her, she'd been engaged to his brother.

"I had my chance."

And he'd blown it. But he couldn't say the words out loud. His regrets were private.

"I understand she's been staying with you in Las Vegas."

"Siggy threatened her, saying he was going to fight for custody of Dylan. I offered her my guesthouse until things could be sorted out."

"Why would Siggy try to take away Dylan?"

"He lost Rafe and saw Dylan as his replacement."

"And he wanted control over the shares of the company that Rafe left his son."

"And he didn't want to pay for them. Rafe left Savannah a lot of debt, and she was trying to sell the label's shares back to Siggy so she could get out from under it."

His mother rolled her eyes. "Tell me you haven't left her to deal with Siggy alone."

"Everything has been sorted out. Another record company offered to buy West Coast Records, so Siggy bought Rafe's shares back and Savannah should be able to pay off her debts. She's moved back to LA and has taken a part in a movie."

Trent decided this was the perfect opportunity to

tell his mother about Dylan being his son, but as he opened his mouth, they were approached by an obviously frazzled man. After his mother introduced her assistant director, they headed off. Trent chose a seat in the dim theater and watched his mother work, enjoying the competent way she directed the actors. It was obvious she had a vision in her head regarding the changes, but it took her an hour and twenty minutes to achieve the results. At long last she clapped her hands and sent everyone on their way.

Collecting her coat and purse, Naomi came up the center aisle toward Trent. "Shall we go to La Masseria for lunch?"

Located in the theater district, the Italian restaurant was one of her favorites. During one of his many trips to visit Savannah, they'd met his mother and her current husband there before a Broadway show. The entire evening had been a great success. His mother had talked about Savannah for months afterward, prodding him about his future plans. Trent had given her noncommittal replies, and as time went on she'd stopped asking questions.

After they were seated, Trent gave the menu a quick glance. He wasn't really hungry. Being in this restaurant brought up happy memories of his time with Savannah, of his mother's hopes for his future and the satisfaction she'd found with a man who supported and loved her.

"Earlier I mentioned that Siggy threatened to seek custody of Dylan, but what I didn't say is that he gave up after discovering that he isn't Rafe's son."

"It sounds just like Siggy." His mother waved to

someone, apparently unconcerned at the bombshell regarding her grandson's legitimacy. "He's obsessed with his legacy."

"Doesn't it bother you about Dylan?"

Naomi met her son's gaze. "Why should it? I love Dylan. Whether or not he's Rafe's biological child doesn't change the fact that he's my grandson." She studied Trent for a long moment. "Does it bother you?"

"It bothers me that Savannah lied."

Why had he thought his mother would be outraged that Savannah had lied, too? Melody hadn't been bothered. Rafe had created the situation in the first place. At this point, the only other member of his family who seemed at all upset was Siggy.

"I don't see why. As you said earlier, you had your chance with her and things didn't work out. It seems as if this is her business and Rafe's. He married her, after all." His mother turned her attention to the waiter who'd approached the table, leaving Trent to stew over her matter-of-fact assessment.

As soon as they'd placed a drink order, Trent spoke again. "It bothers me because Dylan is my son."

"I see." His mother had been perusing a menu she no doubt knew by heart. Now she set it down and gave him her full attention. "Can I assume since you haven't mentioned this before that you just found out?"

"Savannah told me a few days ago."

Naomi laced her fingers together and set her clasped hands on the table. "Does this change things between you?"

"By change things, do you mean am I going to

marry her?" Trent heard his aggrieved tone and saw his mother's eyebrows lift.

"You love her, don't you?"

For some reason the question threw salt on his already raw wounds. "She and I were together a long time. I didn't want to end things, but I couldn't give her the normal family life she craved."

"So marriage is off the table. Do you intend to have a relationship with your son? Or are you going to be like your father?"

If she had stood up and shrieked at him, he would've been less shocked. That she would place him in the same category as his father in anything cut deep. Trent slammed the door on his emotions. Ice filled his veins.

"I haven't decided what I'm going to do."

"Oh, don't be like that." His mother picked up her menu and once more began to peruse the entrées. "Your father used to shut down the exact same way."

"Stop comparing me to him."

"I will when you stop behaving like him. Siggy has no heart and very little soul. He is bullheaded and unforgiving."

"But you married him and had three children. Why do that if he's so terrible?"

"I was young, idealistic and ambitious. He told me I was talented, and I thought with him backing me I would have an amazing career as a singer." Trent's mother sighed. "And in the beginning he charmed the pants right off me."

"What changed?"

"He thought I had an affair."

The waiter brought their drinks, giving Trent a moment to assimilate what his mother had said.

"Did you?"

Naomi didn't look surprised or annoyed by his question. "I didn't sleep with Marco, but I did fall in love with him. He was an incredibly talented musician I met shortly after he signed with West Coast Records."

"Marco? I don't recall anyone by that name at the label."

"That's because your father destroyed his career. He never made an album and eventually gave up music." Naomi got a faraway look in her eye. "It was a year after Rafe was born. Siggy promised that I could record my second album. I'd been working on songs while pregnant with Rafe. One of those was a duet. Marco and I recorded it together. He had the most amazing voice. If he'd signed with any other record company, he probably would've been huge."

Trent couldn't figure out why she was telling him all of this. "Does Siggy think this Marco is my father?" It would explain why he could do no right in his father's eyes. Trent hadn't realize how much he'd needed his father's favoritism to have a basis in logic.

"No. He ran a paternity test on all three of you." Her smile had an acid bite. "That was the moment I stopped trying to make my marriage work. The day I discovered he would never trust me."

"Then why does he hate me?" It was the cry of a small child who didn't understand what he'd done wrong. And it was a question he'd never asked his mother before.

"Because you were my beautiful, musical boy and I

doted on you. Rafe didn't inherit my talent or my joie de vivre. He was a serious baby with the most solemn eyes. It was almost as if from birth he was weighed down by his father's expectations." Trent's mother gave her head a sad shake. "You, on the other hand, and your sister after you, were exuberant and artistic. For all his early success with West Coast Records, Siggy was a businessman, not a visionary. He related better to Rafe."

Trent pondered what he'd learned and realized he'd never stopped being angry with his father. In fact, he'd gone a step farther and used his contentious relationship with his father as an excuse to keep people at bay.

"I don't want to be like my father."

"You're not like him at all."

"So you think I have a heart and a soul?"

His mother smiled. "I never doubted it for a second."

Savannah poured candy into a large bowl and set it on the small table just inside her front door. It was five o'clock on Halloween, but she didn't expect trick-or-treaters to show up for another hour. She and Dylan had been living in LA for a week. The mission-style house she'd rented was about the same size as Trent's guesthouse and beautifully furnished, but Savannah was having a hard time settling in.

She'd had several meetings with the director, her fellow actors and the wardrobe department, and was anxious to start filming. As she'd done after starting the soap opera, she'd hired an acting coach to help her prepare for her new role. But her down time offered abundant opportunity to worry, and lately she'd been revisiting the multitude of ways she could have handled things better since leaving New York two years earlier.

Her doorbell rang. Trick-or-treaters already? Savannah glanced to where her son sat in the middle of the living room, wearing his adorable dragon costume. Seeing that he was occupied with Murphy, also dressed like a dragon, she picked up the bowl of candy and opened her front door.

Instead of an adorable child dressed as a princess or a superhero, a tall, leafy plant with legs stood before her.

"Hello?"

The day before, she'd received a lovely fruit basket from the movie's executive producers, welcoming her on board. She couldn't imagine whom the plant was from.

To her utter shock, the face that emerged from behind the foliage was Trent's.

"I hope it's okay that I dropped by."

Savannah made no move to invite him in. "What are you doing here?"

"I went to New York to visit my mother. She wanted to send you something congratulating you on your new role. I offered to deliver it myself."

"Why would you bother?"

He ignored her blunt question. "Can I come in?"

Reluctantly she stepped back and made a sweeping gesture with her arm. Once Trent and his enormous plant were inside, she put the bowl back on the entry table and closed her front door. Trent looked around the snug living room for a place to set down his burden.

"You don't have a lot of room."

Stunned by his criticism, she crossed her arms over her chest. "It's only Dylan and me. We don't need a lot of space." That said, she stared at him.

"How about if I put it here for now." He set it on the breakfast bar, well out of reach of Dylan's grasp. "I like his dragon costume."

"He's dressed up for Halloween."

"Are you taking him trick-or-treating?"

"We went to the mall yesterday for a Halloween event. Tonight I thought we'd stay home and hand out candy."

"Sounds like fun. Do you want some company?"

She couldn't believe he was standing in her living room, acting as if he didn't wish she'd never come back into his life. Should she confront him on what she had overheard? Her grandmother had often said that those who eavesdrop shouldn't expect to hear good things said about themselves.

"While I appreciate whatever this is you're attempting to do," she began in a severe tone, her broken heart jabbing at her ribs with each breath, "I can't have you popping into and out of our lives anytime you want. I grew up being shuffled between my father and grandmother, and that's not what I want for Dylan. He deserves stability and consistency."

"Is that your way of saying that you don't want me to be part of his life?"

His audacity left her dumbfounded. "Last week you wished you'd never learned the truth."

"I never told you that."

"I overheard you talking to Melody." Savannah's

voice broke. "You don't want to be a father. I get it. Why do you think I didn't tell you in the first place?"

"I was upset. I should never have said that."

"But it's what you felt." And as much as the truth had hurt, she preferred it to the lies Rafe had told her.

"Only for a brief moment. You caught me off guard. All I could think was that you'd kept a huge secret from me, and I couldn't accept that you had your reasons for doing so."

"I'm sorry I didn't tell you right away. I never should have listened to Rafe."

"He told you to keep the truth about Dylan from me?"

"He explained to me about that girl in college." When Trent stared at her blankly, Savannah continued, "The one who got pregnant. You helped her take care of it?"

At last comprehension dawned. "Lisa Wheeler. What does that have to do with our situation?"

"You didn't want to be a father then any more than you do now."

"Wait." Trent raised his hands in a stop gesture. "I didn't get Lisa pregnant. I just helped her. She was a friend. She helped me get a B in a poetry class. We never even dated. She'd been raped and was severely traumatized. I tried to get her to go to the police, but she was from a conservative family and didn't want them to know."

"But why would Rafe..." Savannah's stomach turned over. "He lied to me." And why not. Rafe had deceived her several times before that.

"I had no idea your opinion of me was so low." Trent's lips twitched into a sardonic line.

Perhaps in this instance she'd judged him a little too harshly. "To be fair, you were pretty vocal about your view regarding the whole marriage and kids thing. You didn't want anything to tie you down."

"You were right to listen to Rafe. I gave you no reason to think otherwise. At some point I let my father's negative opinions define me. I figured if I was going to be labeled selfish and no good, I might as well act that way."

"So, what did you hope to gain by coming here?" She didn't understand what he wanted from her. "If you're interested in being part of Dylan's life, I welcome that. I would never keep him from you."

Her son recognized his name and got to his feet. He toddled over to Trent and lifted his arms, asking to be picked up. Savannah's throat tightened as Trent scooped up Dylan and checked out the costume.

"This is really cute. I especially like his horns." Trent's crooked smile had a detrimental effect on Savannah's equilibrium.

She cautioned herself not to read too much into his visit. Just because he'd made an effort to stop by didn't mean his opinions had changed.

Her son was an excellent diversion from her tumultuous emotions. "Dylan, what does the dragon say?"

To her delight Dylan growled, first at her and then his father. Trent laughed.

"I heard you two doing this the night before you left. You were having so much fun. I didn't know how to handle how I was feeling." He lifted Dylan into the air, making him giggle. Trent stared at his son for a long moment, his smile fading. At last he returned his attention to Savannah. "Since then I've had time to think. I want to be part of your life."

"I think that would be great for Dylan." And she meant it.

"What about for you?"

What about her? Having him around all the time would be bittersweet. In her life, but never truly hers.

"I've really missed you." She thought that was safe to admit. But to keep him from getting the wrong idea, she continued, "We were friends for a long time before anything happened between us in New York. It'll be great to be on good terms once again."

"Do you want to go back to being just friends?"

She opened her mouth to say no, but the word couldn't make it past the lump in her throat. The last thing Savannah wanted was to be just friends with Trent, but she couldn't go down that road to heartache again.

He began before speaking again without waiting for her answer. "At one point you thought you'd be okay living in Vegas. Do you still think that's a possibility?"

"We could talk about it. Now that I'm working, my financial situation isn't so dire and I can afford more house there than here."

"And you're okay about traveling back and forth?"

Now that his father was no longer entertaining him, Dylan decided he wanted to be put down and squirmed until Trent set the boy on the floor once more.

"Scarlett has made it work. I don't see why I can't, as well." Savannah watched Dylan head to the bin where she kept his musical train. Plastic clattered as he pulled the pieces out. "My son's happiness is important to me. If living in Las Vegas means you and Dylan get to spend as much time together as possible, then that's what I'll do."

"What about your happiness?"

Since leaving Trent behind and moving to LA she'd discovered peace, but not joy. "I've learned I can be content anywhere as long as I have my family."

"I've learned something, too." He took her hands in his. "The only time I'm happy is when I'm with you."

Savannah stared at Trent while blood pounded in her ears. Had she heard him right? Or was she imagining the words she longed to hear?

"But you said…"

"Forget what I said. I was an idiot. I've been an idiot for a long time. Nothing else explains why I ever let you go." Trent tugged her up against him. "I love you."

A stunned Savannah was marveling at her abrupt turn of fortune even as Trent's lips closed over hers. His kiss reflected all the hunger and longing that filled her. She held on for dear life as her future shifted onto a new track. When at long last he broke the kiss, she was breathless and gloriously happy.

"I love you." His deep voice gave weight to the phrase. "I made the mistake of letting you go once. I can't let that happen again."

Savannah's chest ached at the pain and loss she glimpsed in his gaze. "I'm not going anywhere." She glanced at Dylan, who could not have been less interested in what was going on between his parents. "We are not going anywhere."

"Promise?"

"I promise."

Trent pushed her to arm's length and narrowed his eyes. "I think I need something more concrete than your verbal acceptance."

She laughed. "Do you want it in writing?"

"Absolutely. I demand a legally binding agreement." He reached into his pocket and pulled out a box. He popped the lid and showed her a gorgeous diamond ring. "Will you marry me?"

The engagement ring blurred as tears filled Savannah's eyes. Unable to shake her uncertainty, she whispered, "Are you sure about this?" Her breath stopped as he plucked the ring free of the box and slid it onto her finger.

"I've never been more sure of anything in my life."

"Then, yes." Giddy beyond anything she could imagine, Savannah threw her arms around his neck and hugged him tight. Crushed in his return embrace, she couldn't stop smiling. "I love you so much."

"You and Dylan are my everything. I never want us to be apart ever again."

That brought up a logistical problem. "It's going to be a while until that happens, with me here doing the movie and you in Las Vegas running Club T's."

"I've already got that covered. Both Kyle and Nate are in Vegas for the foreseeable future. Nate plans to get back in the studio, and Kyle has his relationship with my sister to save." He put his arm around her. "I'm going to stay in LA and take care of Dylan while you're working."

That he'd obviously thought this through and was delighted with the prospect lightened her heart. Yet, she remained cautious.

"That's all well and good," Savannah said, appreciating Trent's willingness to throw himself into being Dylan's father, but unsure whether the new role would be enough to satisfy him. "But won't you be bored without some business venture to challenge you?"

"No, because in addition to looking for space for a location for a new club here in LA, I have recently become part owner of a record label in desperate need of help."

"You have?" Something about his self-satisfied expression stirred her suspicions. "You don't mean..."

"Siggy sold the label to Ugly Trout Records. Nate and I now own West Coast Records." Trent's smug grin was difficult to resist, and Savannah found her lips curving in response.

"How?"

"Nate made Siggy an offer he couldn't refuse."

"But you and Nate are business partners in the club. Didn't Siggy realize that?"

"We're also partners in Ugly Trout Records. I helped him with the start-up five years ago."

"Aren't you worried he'll find out you're behind this?"

"Siggy is a bastard. He was so determined to keep me away from West Coast Records that he was willing to dump the company to keep it out of my hands." Trent gave a dismissive shrug. "And anyway, it's too late for him to pull out. The papers are signed."

Savannah smiled as she imagined what her father-in-law's reaction would be when he found out. "He's going to have a fit."

"Too bad. He should have done his research."

"And now you own the company that should have been yours all along." Savannah lifted on tiptoe and brought Trent's lips back to hers for a passionate kiss that left them both breathing hard. "You are clever, talented, and I love you."

Trent's, his smile faded. "I never thought you'd look at me like that ever again."

"Like what?"

"Like I was someone you believed in." He grazed his fingertips across her cheeks and cupped her face. "Ever since I can remember, my father has told me I'm selfish and flawed. He said I would ruin people's lives the way I had ruined his. While I couldn't figure out what I'd done wrong, I accepted that he was right. In the end it became my excuse for the way I'd let you down." He pressed his lips to her forehead. "Every time I saw how I'd disappointed you, I ached for the pain I caused."

"I've always believed in you." Savannah had long known that Siggy was to blame for Trent's commitment issues. "It was believing in us where I lost faith."

An intense glow lit his eyes, transfixing her. "I promise to do everything in my power to make sure that never happens again."

And as he sealed his vow with a slow, reverent kiss, Savannah knew wherever she lived in the future, as long as she was with Dylan and Trent, she would be home.

* * * * *

If you liked this story of a billionaire tamed by the love of the right woman—and her baby—pick up these other novels from Cat Schield

AT ODDS WITH THE HEIRESS
A MERGER BY MARRIAGE
A TASTE OF TEMPTATION
THE NANNY TRAP
ROYAL HEIRS REQUIRED
A ROYAL BABY SURPRISE
SECRET CHILD, ROYAL SCANDAL

Available now from Harlequin Desire!

***

And don't miss the next
BILLIONAIRES AND BABIES *story*

ONE HEIR... OR TWO?

by USA TODAY *bestselling author Yvonne Lindsay*
Available November 2016!

***

If you're on Twitter, tell us what you think of Harlequin Desire! #harlequindesire

Turn your love of reading into rewards you'll love with
Harlequin My Rewards

**Join for FREE today at
www.HarlequinMyRewards.com**

Earn **FREE BOOKS** of your choice.

Experience **EXCLUSIVE OFFERS** and contests.

Enjoy **BOOK RECOMMENDATIONS**
selected just for you.

PLUS! Sign up now
and get **500** points
right away!

Earn
FREE
REWARDS
HarlequinMyRewards.com
Join
Today!

MYR16R

*Rich-as-sin cowboy Sam McCormack wants nothing
to do with ice princess Madison West, but when
they're snowed in together at a mountain retreat,
their red-hot attraction quickly burns through all their
misconceptions…*

*Read on for a sneak peek of
HOLD ME, COWBOY
the latest in Maisey Yates's New York Times bestselling
COPPER RIDGE series!*

"Are you going to suggest that I need *you*?" she asked,
her voice choked.

Lightning streaked through his blood, and in that
moment, he was lost. It didn't matter that he thought
she was insufferable, a prissy little princess who didn't
appreciate anything she had. It didn't matter that he was
up here to work.

All that mattered was he hadn't touched a woman in a
long time, and Madison West was so close all he would
have to do was shift his weight slightly and he'd be able
to take her into his arms.

"Well," he said, "you have a couple of the essential
ingredients to have yourself a pretty fun evening. All you
seem to be missing is a good man. I'm not very nice,
Madison," he said, leaning in, "but I could damn sure
show you a good time."

She should throw him out. She looked over at him, and her libido made a dash to the foreground. That was the problem. He irritated her. He was exactly the kind of man she didn't like. He was cocky; he was rough and crude. However, there was something about the way he looked in a tight T-shirt that made a mockery of all that very certain hatred.

"Are you going to take off your coat and stay awhile?" That question, asked in a faintly mocking tone, sent a dart of tension straight down between her thighs.

She could *not* take off her coat. Because she was wearing nothing more than a little scrap of red lace underneath it. And now it was all she could think of. "It's cold," she snapped. "Maybe if you went to work getting the electricity back on rather than standing here making terrible double entendres I would be able to take off my coat."

The maddening man raised his eyebrows, shooting her a look that clearly said Suit yourself, then set about looking for the fuse box. She let out an exasperated sigh and followed his path, stopping when she saw him leaning against the wall, a little metal door between the logs open as he examined the switches inside.

"It's not a fuse. That means there's something else going on." He slammed the door shut and turned back to look at her. "You should come over to my cabin."

Don't miss
HOLD ME, COWBOY
by New York Times *bestselling author Maisey Yates,*
available November 2016 wherever
Harlequin® Desire books and ebooks are sold.

www.Harlequin.com

Whatever You're Into... Passionate Reads

Looking for more passionate reads from Harlequin®?
Fear not! Harlequin® Presents, Harlequin® Desire and
Harlequin® Blaze offer you irresistible romance stories
featuring powerful heroes.

♦HARLEQUIN *Presents*

Do you want alpha males, decadent glamour and jet-set
lifestyles? Step into the sensational, sophisticated world of
Harlequin® Presents, where sinfully tempting heroes ignite a
fierce and wickedly irresistible passion!

♦HARLEQUIN *Desire*

Harlequin® Desire novels are powerful, passionate and
provocative contemporary romances set against a backdrop of
wealth, privilege and sweeping family saga. Alpha heroes with
a soft side meet strong-willed but vulnerable heroines amid a
dramatic world of divided loyalties, high-stakes conflict and
intense emotion.

♦HARLEQUIN *Blaze*

Harlequin® Blaze stories sizzle with strong heroines and
irresistible heroes playing the game of modern love and lust.
They're fun, sexy and always steamy.

Be sure to check out our full selection of books
within each series every month!

www.Harlequin.com

HPASSION2016